at the
CEMETERY GATES

BRHEL **&** SULLIVAN   YEAR **ONE**

CEMETERY GATES
MEDIA

At The Cemetery Gates: Year One
Published by Cemetery Gates Media
Binghamton, NY

Copyright © 2016 by John Brhel and J. Sullivan

ISBN: 978-1539597759

Printed in the USA by CreateSpace.

For more information about this book and other Cemetery Gates Media publications, visit us at:

cemeterygatesmedia.wordpress.com
cemeterygatesmedia.tumblr.com
facebook.com/cemeterygatesmedia
twitter.com/cemeterygatesm
instagram.com/cemeterygatesm

Cover illustration and design by Chad Wehrle

CONTENTS

At The Cemetery Gates: Year One

INTRODUCTION

Herein lies a collection of beliefs, customs, and lore presented as contemporary cultural entertainment. The following aren't short stories so much as they are digestible suburban fables. In place of talking animals and children's maxims, we've sought to reflect the animal found within the human psyche.

These tales are born of a shared, lifelong interest in the macabre—of summers spent exploring forgotten graveyards and investigating legends, of late-night talk over mothmen and women in white. After years spent in discussion and admiration of anthologized storytelling, we came together in 2015 to pen our first books: *Tales From Valleyview Cemetery* and *Marvelry's Curiosity Shop*. In addition to these themed anthologies, we wrote a number of stories and serials in developing our publishing imprint, Cemetery Gates Media. We have included some of our favorites in this collection, a document of our first year as co-writers.

Strange and supernatural events. Death. Decay. Twisted personae and the unexpected twist. Such subjects have fascinated us for decades, sparked countless legend trips. With this book we aim to conjure in you the same enthusiastic joy—odd as it may seem—in the dark and unknown.

John and Joe
October 2016

At The Cemetery Gates: Year One

A DARK AND DESOLATE RECURRENCE

"At this rate, we'll never get out of here," said Teddy Mealer, gritting his teeth as he yanked the steering wheel of his compact car and laid on the gas. His Prius, as it turned out, wasn't built for blizzard-level conditions in the Catskills, and he was reminded of it every time his engine roared in a vain attempt to retreat from the large snowbank.

"Don't say that, honey," replied his wife, Margo. She looked out in fear at the snow piled up against her window. It was a vision of white on all sides of the car; each window was suffocated by snow, with only a hint of an opening out of the rear window.

"I don't think you understand, babe. I can't move. I think we're stuck here."

A panicked look crossed Margo's face. "Are you serious?" She nudged the handle on her door, then proceeded to yank it and kick at the door before her husband restrained her.

Teddy shook his head. "You're wasting your time. I'll keep trying, but I don't think it'll do any good. We're packed like sardines."

Nearly another half-hour passed and Teddy was unable to free the car from the clutches of the cold, white mass. He punched the steering wheel in frustration. "We're nearly out of gas. We've got to get out of here soon or we'll freeze. Or worse, there's the whole carbon monoxide thing."

Margo took her cell phone out of her purse for the third time in the past ten minutes, but she couldn't get a signal. "Teddy, I'm scared. What are we going to do?"

"I don't know." There was a newfound weariness to his voice, as if the dread that his wife was experiencing had finally caught up to him.

Margo was about to throw a fit when she heard the roar of another engine. She looked outside to see the headlights of a large, black pickup with an attached plow pull up behind their car. The front door opened and out stepped a bearded, middle-aged man in a brown parka and dungarees.

"Ted, I think this guy's going to help us out!" Margo beamed. She took her husband's hand and squeezed it in excitement.

"Thank god."

They watched as the man took a chain and attached it somewhere underneath their car. He returned to his truck and gunned it in reverse. Teddy and Margo let out a mutual sigh of relief as their car creaked back and forth stubbornly, before slipping out of the snowbank and onto the road.

The man got out of his truck again, detached the chain from their car, and threw it back onto the bed. He stopped and looked inside at the couple for a brief second before getting into his vehicle. Teddy and Margo watched as their Good Samaritan drove away.

"What a nice man," said Margo. "He didn't even ask for anything. Didn't even wait around for a thank-you."

"People out here look out for each other," said Teddy. "That's a good guy, there."

Teddy went to drive away, but the car wouldn't move. They were out of the bank, but the vehicle was immobile. "Son of a bitch! What now?"

Margot was agonizingly silent.

"It feels like the rear axle might be broke. Shit— why'd that guy have to leave in such a hurry? I mean, he was a big help and all, but where'd he go?" said Ted. He forced his door open and looked down the road, but all he could see was a dense, white snow fog. He examined the rear of the car and, sure enough, the wheel was crooked because the axle was broken.

Teddy returned to the car and sighed. With their gas tank almost empty, the couple decided that they would have to leave the Prius behind and seek shelter. They stepped out of the vehicle and were instantly struck by the frigid, winter air. They walked for only a minute before they noticed a small cabin set back a few hundred yards from the road. They decided to head for it and ask whoever lived there if they could come inside. It was beginning to grow dark, so they trudged onward into the foot-high snow.

Teddy and Margo arrived at a modest cabin. There was a small porch attached to the front, on which sat Adirondack chairs, snow piled up on each seat. A wide, stone chimney jutted out just off to one side of the porch, many of the stones having fallen to the ground nearby. They stepped onto the porch and wood cracked beneath their feet.

Teddy knocked repeatedly on the door, but no one answered. He turned the doorknob and felt that it wasn't locked.

He called out before they ventured inside. "Hello? Is anybody home?"

No one answered. The icy wind howled through the evergreens behind them.

"I guess not," said Margo.

The cold snapping against their faces, the couple had no other option but to enter. As they passed through the doorway, they were immediately taken aback by a sharp musty smell.

"*Ugh*, Teddy. That *smell*. Who the heck lives here? Don't they clean?"

"I don't think anyone's lived here for years. Or it might be a poorly kept hunting cabin—this is deer country, after all," said Teddy. He looked around. They were standing in a small living room which had a loft area above. There was a TV and a sofa, which was adorned with a blanket, on which was stitched a grey wolf howling at the moon. A large mirror hung over the sofa.

The living room led into a kitchen with a modest-sized refrigerator and stove, and a table for two. The kitchen had the sole working light on the first floor, which hung from a string, and shone into the living room. Cobwebs covered every corner and piece of furniture in the cabin; crunchy leaves and various forest debris were scattered about the floor.

"It's like they just ran out and left everything behind," said Margo.

Teddy found a book of matches inside a kitchen drawer and used it to light a fire in a small wood stove in the corner of the living room. Kindling and enough wood for the night was conveniently set near the entranceway. He took a seat next to Margo on the sofa and they held each other, warming up until the room was a bearable temperature.

Worn out from their ordeal on the road and the trek to the cabin, they quickly passed out on the stranger's sofa.

Margo wasn't asleep twenty minutes when she tapped Teddy on the shoulder. "What's that noise?"

There was a heavy pounding on the loft floor above, as if someone were stomping around. They listened with intense curiosity as one set of footsteps traveled down from the loft, followed by a second, heavier set.

Margo tucked her head into her husband's shoulder. "Oh, my god, somebody's inside. Maybe the owners came home."

"Don't you think they would have come in through the front door? Maybe saw us on the couch and woke us up? Why would they be running up and down the steps?" said Teddy. "It might be some rats, or raccoons, or something. Who knows what openings or broken windows there might be in an old, forgotten place like this."

Teddy was about to lay his head back against the cushion when he heard what was unmistakably a human scream. It was that of a woman, and she kept repeating the same word in a frenzied tone, over and over. "*No, no, no!*"

Neither Teddy nor Margo moved. The screaming continued, traveling from upstairs to downstairs, growing louder, more intense with each passing minute. This continued for another ten minutes, when suddenly, as if someone had flicked a switch, it stopped. No more screaming, no more footsteps. The sound gone, all they could hear was the creaking of the house and the whistling of the wind outside.

"*What was that?!*" whispered Margo, her face tense.

"I don't know. It sounded like someone being chased around. But I didn't see a thing."

"Teddy, is this place *haunted?*" Margo couldn't believe she was asking such a question, or that she half-considered it to be a possibility.

They discussed leaving the cabin for a moment but realized they still couldn't venture outside. Not at least until morning. The snowfall had waned, but the wind had picked up quite considerably.

Hungry, they searched the kitchen for food. Margo opened the refrigerator and nearly vomited at the pungent, death-like smell that wafted out. Undefined molds lined the drawers and compartments. She quickly slammed the door.

Teddy had a little more luck. He managed to scrounge up a couple cans of fruit cocktail from a lower cabinet that were less than a year past expiration. He found a can opener and they shared the meager portion.

Their bellies as full as they would get for the night, and the cabin now comfortably warm, Teddy and Margo climbed the stairs to the loft to explore. The closet light held the only working bulb in the loft, and it shone a comfortable glow into the bedroom. The bed was unmade, and it looked as if the sheets had been thrown on the floor in a fit. A pair of panties and a pair of boxers were strewn with some other faded articles of clothing.

"It looks like a couple lives here. Or should I say 'lived' here," said Teddy.

They flipped the mattress and dug a clean, moth-bitten bedsheet out from a dresser, then laid down together. They were sound asleep minutes later.

"No! No! Oh, god, no! It doesn't mean anything! I love you! Oh, please don't hurt him!"

Margo let out an awful cry as she awoke, the shrill woman's voice again echoing throughout the cabin. She looked at her husband's watch. She and Teddy hadn't been sleeping twenty minutes.

"What the fuck *is* that?" asked Teddy. "I'm going to check it out."

"No," said Margo, throwing herself over her husband. "Please don't leave me."

This time, they heard the pounding all around them, coming from the staircase and traveling toward the bed. The couple screamed as the bed lifted off the ground a few inches and crashed back down to the floor. The footsteps traveled from the loft and all the way down to the kitchen, and possibly the basement. This time, the chaos ended with a loud "*ka-pow*," as if someone had fired a gun. Then another "*ka-pow*." Then silence.

Tears streamed down Margo's face. "Let's go. Oh, god, let's get out of here!" She ran out of the bed and down the stairs, ready to bolt out the front door, but Teddy chased after her and blocked the doorway.

"Where are you going?" he asked.

"Ted, this place is haunted. I'm scared!"

He held her tight by the shoulders and nodded. "Okay, okay. I believe you. I think it's haunted, too. Some repetitive haunting is going on here. Every hour or so. I heard about this kind of thing watching all those seasons of *Ghost Stalkers*. Someone who dies under extreme circumstances often ends up repeating the events leading up to their death, over and over again. I think someone was murdered here, and it's playing out like the cabin has the awful memory imprinted on it."

"Then let's go! Why are you standing there if you know what's coming!"

"Because it's a goddamn blizzard out there, and we'll die if we spend an hour in it. It's two in the morning and we're miles from anywhere. Nobody's going to stop by. That nice guy with the truck is long gone."

"So what do we do, Teddy?"

"I don't think the ghosts can harm us. They're dead and simply re-enacting a scene; we're just observers. Those poor bastards. Could you imagine being forced to re-live the same horrible event forever?"

Realizing the bed in the loft played a major part in the haunting, Teddy convinced Margo to return to the couch on the first floor. They weren't going to get much sleep anyway.

Each hour, the haunting commenced. The bed in the loft, the pounding footsteps descending downstairs to the kitchen, through the living room. Then the two gunshots. But Teddy and Margo weren't safer in the living room, as it turned out. As the night wore on, more chaos unfolded. They watched in horror as objects flew across the room—clothes, pillows, books. They were forced to duck and dive as heavier objects arced through the air—a lamp, dishes, at one point a small television.

Teddy held close to Margo beneath the wolf blanket; they were too frightened to keep stoking and tending to the fire. They both shivered as each hour the horrors seemingly escalated. It was a form of torture, one they dreaded more as each minute passed, knowing that the next repetition would be more intense, more violent.

Teddy was nodding off during one of the lulls between repetitions, the sun just beginning to make its presence known through the dirty windows, when Margo let out a wild scream. He watched as his wife was lifted into the air. She clutched at her throat, trying to tear away an invisible set of hands. Her face was straining and turning a shade of purple. He jumped up and threw his body into the phantom perpetrator. Teddy connected with the unseen force and Margo fell to the floor, gasping for air.

Teddy looked up and saw the reflection of a man running away in the mirror over the couch. Although it was dark, with a little light from the bulb in the kitchen, he could have sworn it was the same man in the brown parka and dungarees that had helped tow their car out of the snowbank.

Footsteps pounded down to the basement again. The two gunshots that ended it all, but this time a third shot rang out, just minutes later.

That was all the Mealers could take. They ran outside as the orange rays of the sun began peeking over the mountains. The storm had died down and the air was noticeably warmer.

"I think I figured out what happened," said Teddy, out of breath from his exertion. "The man who lived there killed his wife. The underwear on the floor? I think he caught her in bed with another man and chased them around the house. It all ended in the basement, where he shot them both and then himself—the third shot."

Margo nodded in silence as they swiftly left the cabin behind, postholing through the deep snow. She didn't care who killed who; she just wanted to go home.

"I think the guy with the pickup was the one who killed them," stated Teddy. "Honey, I think we got pulled out of a ditch by a *ghost*."

They made it back to the road, hoping they could flag down a passing motorist and hitch a ride into town. As they neared the scene of their accident, they were surprised to see the car was no longer sitting where they had abandoned it—it was firmly lodged in the snowbank. They stopped dead in their tracks when it was clear the same black pickup from the night before was pulling their Prius free.

"Honey, that ghost. He's back again," said Teddy.

They stood silently, watching as the man in the brown parka and dungarees exited his truck to retrieve the chains. The man then looked into the driver-side window of their car, shook his head and jogged back toward his truck—shouting back over his shoulder, "I live just up ahead. I'll go call an ambulance!"

Margo and Teddy walked over to the Prius as the truck tore down the road. They couldn't believe their eyes. There they were, sitting in the front seat, their faces ghastly white. They were dead, long dead.

"Teddy. What?! Who are these people?" Margo's lip quivered. A nasty wind whipped against her face. "They look like…"

"Us! That's because it *is* us, honey. We're dead. That guy was the killer. See him driving away? He's going to go find his wife in bed with another man and kill them both. Don't you see? He returned home early because he was going to go call us an ambulance. He didn't know we were dead. We're just like him, repeating our episode."

At The Cemetery Gates: Year One

A CASKET FOR MY MOTHER

Craig Donnelly was finally back at his parents' house and settling in, having just returned from a two-year stint as an English teacher in China. His bedroom was just as he had left it after college. He sat down at his desk and turned on his old computer. When he opened his web browser he was surprised to find that he was still signed into Facebook.

The village where Craig taught didn't have Wi-Fi, and even when he could get online his regular email client, and the social media sites he frequented, were blocked by the government. He had dozens of private messages waiting for him. Some were from friends who were wondering where he had gone, others from family messaging him in hopes that he might log on at some point in his travels. Craig didn't bother reading more than a few of the messages, as he was more interested in getting a sense of what was happening in the present.

He scrolled down his timeline, passing over news stories, celebrity gossip, advertisements, and political hodgepodge—nothing of any interest to a man who had been abroad for years. What gave him pause was a GoFundMe post from his old friend

Tim Burns. The funding request was titled: 'A Casket for My Mother.' The brief summary simply read, *Help me pay for a casket for my recently deceased mother.*

Craig was shocked to discover that Tim's mom had passed and that his own parents hadn't mentioned it when they picked him up from the airport that morning. Their families had been close growing up and throughout high school, and had only lost touch when both boys went to separate universities. But Craig had stayed in contact with Tim via social media in the intervening years, and certainly felt for his friend when he read of his mother's death.

He shared Tim's GoFundMe post and wrote him a message: *"I'm sorry to hear about your mother. Let me know if there's anything I can do to help."*

Minutes later, Craig received a message from Tim thanking him for his kind words. Craig told his old friend about his teaching gig in China, that he had only come home that morning and didn't know Tim's mother had died until he opened his computer.

"She was a nice woman, and I only have good memories of her from when we were young. She treated me like I was her own kid," wrote Craig. *"I'm sorry we haven't kept in touch the past couple years. I was in a really rural part of China and there was no real access to the internet."*

"Thanks, Craig. I hope you get a chance to stop by and see us. I miss hanging out with you," replied Tim.

"Well, I don't have much going on this afternoon. If you're free, I'd love to stop by."

Tim told Craig to stop over whenever he had the time.

Later that day, Craig pulled into Tim's driveway and saw that his friend was out trimming the hedges. Craig hopped out of the car and the pair greeted each other warmly, hugging and laughing. They chatted for the next half hour about what each had been up to, what they had in mind for their immediate futures, and how Tim had been dealing with his loss.

An odd combination of smells (citrus and vinegar) wafted around Craig as they talked and laughed about old memories. He didn't think much of the strange smells, at the time, and fished out his checkbook. "Hey, let me write you a check toward the casket."

At first Tim resisted, but he didn't put up much of a fight when Craig insisted. Craig searched his pockets for a pen. When he realized he had forgotten to bring a pen, Tim said he'd go grab one, and ran up the porch steps and into the house.

While Craig waited, he took out his phone and saw that he had a private message from his and Tim's mutual friend, Adam. *"Dude, I saw that you shared Tim's GoFundMe page. Have you actually read it? I think he's running a scam."*

Confused, Craig opened the GoFundMe page. The request had been active for 33 days and $0 had been raised. He thought it odd that no one had donated. He read the description: *"My mother has suddenly passed and I can't afford a proper casket for her burial. Please help me purchase a casket for my mother. There are many great perks for the different tiers. She was a wonderful woman and mother."*

It all seemed like a fairly normal crowdfunding request, until he scrolled down to the perks.

Donate $5 and you will have my mother's eternal thanks.
Donate $10 and you will receive a flower from my mother's grave, plus previous tier.
Donate $20 and you will receive a piece of my mother's burial linen, plus previous tiers.
Donate $40 and you will receive a lock of my mother's hair, plus previous tiers.

Craig found the page slightly morbid, but it wasn't entirely out of character for Tim to be unaware of social norms and etiquette; he had always been a somewhat strange character. Still, it didn't make sense why neither Adam nor any of his other friends had pledged.

He messaged Adam: *"Yeah, it's a bit weird, but why hasn't anyone donated yet?"*

Craig was waiting for Adam's response when Tim called out to him from behind the screen door. "I found a pen, man. Come on in!"

He went up and into the house, feeling bad that nobody had given Tim any money toward his mother's funerary casket. When he stepped through the door he was taken aback by an odd sight. Dozens of air fresheners were stuck to the walls and even the ceiling. Lemon-scented chemicals assaulted Craig's nose and he almost had to step back outside to get some air.

But he pushed forward, following Tim into the parlor, which looked exactly as it had when they were kids. Even the TV had yet to be upgraded to a flat screen. Tim handed him a pen and Craig began writing out a check for $100.

"So, is your mom still at the morgue? That's gotta be expensive in itself," said Craig, making small talk. "I can't imagine insurance would pay much toward that."

"No!" said Tim, snickering.

Craig looked up at his friend, bewildered by his reaction. "Then where is she?"

Tim turned and called upstairs: "Mother! Craig's here. He'd like to see you." The room was silent as both pairs of ears listened for a response as if it would naturally come. "Mother?!"

Craig shook his head as if to clear it from his sudden confusion.

"Just a minute, man," said Tim before running upstairs. Craig froze, unable to process exactly what was occurring. He listened intently as Tim stomped up the two separate flights of stairs and into the room above. He heard some shuffling, grunting, and then something heavy being dragged across the floor. Soon there was a *bump, bump, bump* as the mass was pulled down the stairs, followed by a loud *thud* in the landing.

Craig was shaken from his daze and ran from the house, just as Tim was turning the corner in the landing with whatever he was about to bring down the lower set of stairs and into the parlor.

While Craig sped back home he pulled out his phone, wondering whether or not he should call the police on his old friend, or try and forget the whole thing and never talk to him again. He saw that Adam had responded to his previous message.

"Dude, she died over a year ago... I was at her funeral. I told him he should just get her cremated, but he insisted she wanted to be buried. They charged him an arm and a leg for that crappy plywood box they stuck her in. We pitched in what we could."

When Craig got home he blocked Tim on Facebook, on his phone, and on every other mode of communication he could think of. He needed some time to process what had occurred.

Days later, he received a small, unmarked package in the mail. Inside lay a withered white lily, a piece of soiled linen, a lock of hair, and a thank-you note—signed by Tim's mother, with her eternal gratitude.

TIME'S HARBINGER

With apprehension, Ross Everett pulled his car up to a drab apartment building, where his father, Gary, stood awkwardly. The aging man was dressed in a cheap pair of black slacks, a black tie, and a white dress shirt—funeral attire.

Gary opened the back door and tossed his threadbare sports jacket on the seat. He greeted his son with a put-on grin as he climbed into the passenger seat; Ross was immediately irked by the cigarette smell clinging to Gary's clothes. They headed north, forcing out the minimum of conversation.

"So how you keeping up in New York, big shot? I heard you got a job in advertising?" asked Gary.

"That's right," mumbled Ross, a response that typified his interaction with his father.

"You like it?"

Ross kept his eyes focused on the road. "Yeah."

Gary picked up the rosary that sat in Ross' cup holder and inspected it. "Your mother's rosary, right?"

Ross snatched it from his father and stuck it in his pants pocket. "Yep. She's going to be buried with it."

An uncomfortable silence settled in the car for the remainder of the drive. It had been 25 years since Gary stormed out of their small house in

Otisville, NY, leaving Ross and his mother, Karen, to fend for themselves. Time had yet to heal the wound this incident left on Ross, who was just eight at the time. Gary appeared sporadically throughout his son's life. Noteworthy occasions included a Little League game and a ten-minute heartfelt conversation at Ross' 21st birthday party—but for the most part, the man was a ghost.

Ross and his mother had moved downstate not two years after Gary's departure, to start anew, and Karen's sister Jennie had taken possession of the property. But Karen held a fondness for the village and stated in her will that she wished to be buried there. Pancreatic cancer made that happen sooner than she or Ross would have ever expected.

Without a vehicle, and wishing to pay his final respects to his first love and the mother of his child, Gary asked his son if he could grab a ride. Ross, given the situation, felt unable to refuse—thought he had wanted to.

They drove for an hour in near silence until they crossed the bridge leading into Otisville.

"When did they build *this* bridge?" asked Gary.

"Right around the time you left," said Ross. "There was a nasty accident and the old bridge came down."

A few moments later, they passed by the ruins of the former bridge. A corroded hunk of the truss jutted out over the Shawangunk Kill. A concrete barrier stood in front, blocking any troublemakers.

"Do you remember when you were a kid and people used to say they saw the Jersey Devil perched up on it?"

A slight grin crept over Ross' face. "Yeah, but it wasn't the Jersey Devil. They called it Griselphet. I was obsessed with that story from about age ten to twelve. I read everything I could find out about it."

"*Haha*. That's right. That guy Paul Petrosky wrote a book about it. He was even in *The Post* talking about it."

"Paul's book was my Bible. I think I still have my signed copy somewhere," said Ross, thinking fondly of his childhood explorations around the bridge and into the woods on the far side of the creek. "I watch all the monster and legend investigation shows they come out with now, waiting for them to do something on the Demon of Otisville. Nothing so far. It might be too derivative of the Jersey Devil."

They continued to chat and discovered they had seen many of the same ghost hunting and legend-tripping TV shows. It was the first real conversation they'd had in nearly a decade.

Gary gazed out the window as they neared a drive-in movie theater. "Ha. The drive-in! Looks like it's still in business. Can you believe that?"

Ross turned around to get a quick view of the theater which, sure enough, appeared like it was still active. The lot looked freshly sealed and the tall sign outside listed a double feature of *Big Trouble in Little China* and *Labyrinth*. "Maybe drive-ins are making a comeback. Look at the movies; they're doing some kind of 80s revival."

"You know, your mom and I used to go to that drive-in back when we were dating. Even then I remember it was pretty rundown," reminisced Gary. "God, those were the days."

Ross shuffled in his seat, but didn't respond to his father. The fewer reminders of the past, the better, he thought.

"When's the last time you talked to your Aunt Jennie?" asked Gary.

"Other than yesterday, I saw her at a family reunion in Middletown about six months back."

"A family reunion, huh?"

Ross nodded.

Gary attempted to fill the void. "So how's the house looking? She taking good care of it?"

"I don't know. I haven't been back in years." Ross' attention was drawn to a series of vintage cars passing by. "There must be a classic car show in town."

Gary turned to see a line of old cars whizz by—a '76 Plymouth Duster, an '82 Camaro, and a restored Dodge Rampage caught his eye. "Those bring back some memories. I had a white Firebird for a few years, before you were born. Such a clean-looking car."

"Why'd you get rid of it?"

"Couldn't keep up with the loan," replied Gary. "Your mother and I weren't the best with money. It's gotta be the number-one thing that wrecks marriages. Always coming up short at the end of the month."

"I remember Mom being pretty damn *good* with money, actually. It was hard, but she always got us through."

Gary didn't immediately respond; he was all too familiar with his son's baiting tone. As Ross turned onto Highland Avenue and then State Street, they looked out their separate windows and silently recalled some of their old haunts.

"I think I remember the way to the funeral home, but we gotta stop and get gas first; I'm on E." Ross pulled into a Texaco service station.

"I'll pay. Least I can do," stated Gary, firmly. "You want a drink or something?"

Ross nodded then began pumping, while Gary went inside for a couple of Cokes. His father returned, popping the caps off with his keychain then handing one of the glass bottles to his son.

"Look at that, Ross, real Coke bottles. Don't see these too often anymore."

"Thanks," said Ross, taking the soda. "This town is something else. The gas station, hardware store, and market all look exactly the same. Like nothing's changed."

"That's Otisville. No reason to come through really, unless you live here. Your mother practically had to drag me up Old Mountain Road."

Ross wasn't amused. "Yep, no reason for anyone to come up here, or New Hampton, or Goshen, apparently," said Gary, listing the towns where had lived as a boy which his father had rarely visited.

"She didn't want me around. I did the best I could. I sent any extra money I could scrape together…" replied Gary. "I didn't do half as good in school as you, could never get any real promotion in construction or with the cable company."

"You're full of shit, Dad," said Ross as he finished pumping and slammed the fuel flap shut.

Gary puffed away at his cigarette. "There will always be lifelong ditch diggers, Son. There's nothing wrong with that. I was never an alcoholic or addict—never hit a woman or went to jail. Even worked as a volunteer firefighter for a couple years."

"Congratulations on your mediocrity." Ross tossed his half-finished Coke into the trash and drove away before Gary had time to react.

"I guess I'll head over to your aunt's house then," called out Gary to no one in particular, as Ross' car had already rounded a corner. He began the short walk toward his old home, wondering what could possibly have upset his son.

Ross sped down the road, fueled by two decades-worth of disappointment. His old man could find his own way around town, he thought. And besides, it felt good to show him what it's like to be left behind.

He pulled into the parking lot at Farrell Funeral Home and checked his watch—it was 1 p.m., time for his appointment. He went up to the wide front door and knocked. The door opened and a dark-haired man in a grey business suit appeared.

"Can I help you?" asked the man, who seemed slightly perturbed.

"Hi, I'm here to handle the arrangements for my mother, Karen Kroft. Her funeral is tomorrow. I'm her son."

The man looked puzzled. "I'm sorry. There are no funerals planned for tomorrow. And there is no deceased here by that name."

Ross glanced back at the large, wooden sign on the front lawn. The words 'Farrell Funeral Home' stood out in big golden letters. "What do you mean? My mother is supposed to be here."

"I'm sorry, young man. You are mistaken. There is no one by that name here."

"Are there any other funeral homes in town?" asked Ross, who felt unnerved by this strange turn of events. "My aunt set up the appointment."

The man shook his head. "I'm sorry. I am the only licensed mortician in Otisville."

"Oh," said Ross, not quite sure how to react to this information. He took out his cellphone and searched through the texts his aunt had sent him concerning the funeral. It was as he had thought: it was scheduled to take place at Farrell Funeral Home.

"Perhaps your aunt was mistaken. Families tend to get emotional in times of death. Maybe she meant the Richards Family Funeral Home over in Cuddebackville? You can use the phone inside if you'd like." The man made a motion for Ross to step through the door.

"I've got my own," Ross snapped back. This was crazy, he thought. This was his mother's *body* for god's sake. He attempted to call his aunt but found that his cell phone had no reception. "Goddamn podunk town!"

The undertaker backed into the doorway, eyeing Ross peculiarly.

"Can you check with someone else inside?"

"There is *no one* else to consult." The man's voice had taken on a sharper tone. "I am the director, and I can say with 100-percent certainty that your mother is not here. *Good day.*"

The door shut with a heavy thud. Ross stood there incredulously.

As Gary neared his former home, he was surprised to see that the name Everett was still painted on the side of the mailbox. The house, considering its age, was as attractive and quaint as he remembered. The tire swing that he used to push Ross on hung invitingly from the pear tree out front.

Gary was about to cross the street toward the property when he heard screaming coming from inside the house and watched the porch screen door swing open violently. He paused, captivated by the scene, and his eyes went wide when he saw the man stumbling out of the house and onto the front lawn. It appeared to be *him*, though 25 years his junior. The same blue eyes, flat nose, and big chin, but about thirty pounds lighter and a full head of brown hair.

"You good-for-nothin' bitch!" yelled the young man, as he pointed back at the house.

Gary then spotted the focus of his doppelganger's ire. It was his ex-wife, Karen, glowering at her current husband from the doorway. He had really only seen her in pictures in the intervening years, and he was taken aback by the sight of the young and vital woman he once loved.

His eyes were then drawn to the second-floor window, where another ghost from his past appeared. There stood an eight-year-old boy, crying in the frame of the window as his father lumbered toward the car. Gary didn't recall seeing Ross in the window at the time; he had been too consumed with rage.

Gary wasn't sure what was happening—if he was experiencing some form of hallucination—but he was moved to run toward the car and stop his younger self from driving off. Unfortunately, it was too late. The other Gary had already floored it, and the Buick sped down the road, never to return.

Gary was openly sobbing when another car pulled up to the curb in front of him. It was Ross.

"Dad! You're not going to believe this. I went to the funeral home and they said Mom's body wasn't there. Aunt Jennie must have written down the wrong funeral home." Ross stopped when he noticed his father's face was wet with tears. "*Dad?*"

"I'm sorry, Son," said Gary, embracing Ross, who stood still, unsure what had inspired such a wellspring of emotion.

"Dad...what's going on?"

Gary didn't respond, but instead pointed across the street toward their old house, letting the scene before them serve as his explanation.

Ross turned and saw the same image that had made his father's jaw drop only moments before. Karen was still framed in the doorway, but now she was crying as she glared down the empty road after her husband. Ross stood silent, mouthing something to himself, but no words came out.

"Son, I can't explain it, but I think this is 1986— the day I left."

Ross remained fixated on the specter of his young mother.

"Mom's not at the funeral home because she's not dead...at least not yet," said Gary.

Ross started to walk toward the woman, but Gary grabbed him by the arm and held him back.

"No! You shouldn't..."

"What do you mean? Mom's alive! I'm going to see her!"

Across the street, an old man came out from his house and stared. It was Mike Bauman, retired grist mill worker. Other neighbors had poured out of their homes, too, to get a good look at the hollering going on over at the Everett home. Not like they weren't used to screaming coming from that way. Karen, too, noticed the strange men in the street.

Gary kept his grip. "I don't think that's a good idea, Son. I don't know what's happening, but I don't think we're supposed to be here."

There was a rustling in the trees not far above, which caught their attention. A few leaves fluttered to the ground, and the branches shook as if a flock of birds had just landed. While Gary was looking up,

Ross freed himself from his father's grasp. "Let go of me. Maybe *you* don't care about her, but I do!"

Ross started toward the house but stopped when he felt a strange sensation throughout his body, as if some invisible force were holding him back. His feet seemed to sink into the warm pavement. At the same time, his vision became blurry, the air around him somehow exceedingly humid. He felt a presence surrounding him, something incorporeal but aware.

At that moment, a large shadow passed over Ross and his father, and they were both taken aback by the sight of an opaque being materializing on the roof of their old home.

Gary, sensing that something was seriously wrong, grabbed a dazed Ross and dragged him to the car. They sped away, without looking back.

"Son, are you alright?" Gary accelerated down the road, checking in the rearview mirror for sign of the hazy figure.

Ross was pale and listless. He explained the strange sensations to his father and began to come to terms with the possibility they had traveled back to 1986. He recalled what he had read in *Angels of the New Order*, a popular book written by Paul Petrosky. Ross recalled the lore about the Griselphet, rattling off its mythos with a renewed energy. That the creature was a harbinger of time, an angel of wrath, its task that of destruction rather than renewal. And it appeared that Ross and his father were its latest target.

Gary and Ross agreed that they needed to get out of town, and fast. They drove past the Texaco station and the familiar shops and sites.

"Look, Ross, the new bridge is gone, but the old one is still standing! This *has* to be the past..." Gary weaved around a slow-moving tow truck, determined to cross the bridge and leave the town and past behind. But as they turned toward the entrance they were startled by a blinding white light and the reappearance of the opaque being, blocking their way.

Ross again felt the influence of some strange, intangible force over his person, and this time Gary experienced it as well. Their body heat shot up and a wave of terrible nausea passed over the father and son.

Gary fought the sensation, quickly correcting his course and swerving back onto the main road.

"What the hell is happening?!" said Ross.

"I don't know," replied Gary, nervously. He continued to drive, unsure of their next step.

"What *was* that thing?"

"You saw it, too?" said Gary, who had thought it was a figment of his imagination.

"Yep."

After a momentary pause, Ross suddenly blurted out "Paul!"

"Huh?" Gary turned his eyes from the road briefly.

"We need to find Paul Petrosky. If anyone will know what's going on, he will."

Gary, who had no better ideas, nodded. "I used to see him at the Octagon Inn—it's only a block or two away."

After a few turns, Gary and Ross were parked beside a newer blue Chevy El Camino in front of the Octagon Inn.

"Shit, that's Digger's car..." mumbled Gary as they got out and walked toward one of his old watering holes.

When they opened the door to the bar, Ross coughed a couple of times, having not been in contact with that volume of smoke since he was a kid. The Octagon was cramped, dark, and dirty. He looked around at the ripped-open bar stools, the riffraff seated around the bar, and thought of all the nights his father had spent there while he and his mother sat at home, wondering.

"Holy shit! How can people breathe in here?" asked Ross, as he waved his hand in front of his face.

His father grinned, momentarily forgetting about their predicament and soaking up the past. He wandered over to the pool table and ran his hand over the felt. Gary was startled from his reminiscence when someone called out, "Hey, Everett!" He turned, expecting to greet a long-forgotten friend.

Ross shuddered when the fifty-something fire chief seemed to recognize not Gary, but him. He had known the man's son well, and had been at the chief's wake a few days before Christmas in 1987.

"Oh, hell. I'm sorry, buddy. I thought you were goddamn Gary Everett..." The intoxicated fire chief trailed off and returned to his barstool.

Gary watched as the men in the bar eyed his son, some squinting as if making sure it wasn't actually Gary they were looking at. He went over to the bar as his son began to question the bartender.

"Sir, do you know a Paul Petrosky?" asked Ross.

"Nope, don't think so," replied the barman as he filled a glass with a frothing cup of beer.

Ross looked back at his father, unsure of what they should do.

The fire chief had overheard the exchange. "Hey, guy, did you say 'Petrosky?'"

"Yes, Chief. Paul. Scrawny guy with glasses," stated Gary.

The chief turned to eye Gary, squinting at him for a moment before responding. "Yeah. Dick Petrosky and his boy live on Seybolt. Big red brick house."

"Thanks, Chief," replied Gary while nudging his son to let him that know they should leave the bar immediately.

As the door closed behind Gary and Ross, the chief called out, asking where he knew them from. They didn't turn back but rushed to the car and got back onto the road.

"Ha! They thought you were me," said Gary, inspecting his son.

"We have to find Paul," replied Ross, who was focused on getting to Seybolt Ave. as quickly as possible. "I can't be stuck in 1986. Jesus Christ."

They arrived at the Petrosky house and hurried to the front door. It was a worn brick two-family, not the kind of place where you would expect a bestselling author to reside. Ross rang the doorbell and the two waited, anxiously.

The door opened moments later. Ross was surprised to find that Paul was a rather mild-mannered, buttoned-up academic type, and not the frazzled stoner he had met as a teenager at a horror convention in Tarrytown.

"Hi, can I help you?" asked Paul.

"Mr. Petrosky?" asked Gary.

"Yes?" He appeared surprised to have visitors.

"What do you know about time travel?"

Paul chuckled, looking up and down the street to see if he was being made a fool. "Are you screwing with me? I know people around here think I'm crazy, but—"

"We're not screwing with you," said Ross, stepping in front of his father. "We have a serious problem and you're the only one in town who could possibly help."

"Come in," said Paul warily, yet curiously.

Paul took the Everett men into his father's home and they attempted to explain the entirety of the situation to him. At first the amateur demonologist was skeptical of their story, but they seemed so genuine, and legitimately fearful, that he gave them the benefit of the doubt. He guided Ross and Gary to another room, which was filled with books, candles, and various religious and demonic iconography. Paul retrieved a dark manuscript and then opened a small cabinet, retrieving a cross with arms dividing into three sharp points.

"This is a Coptic Cross. May it afford you safe passage over the bridge," said Paul, solemnly. "The being you describe is unlike any I have encountered or studied. Its connection to time seems rather angelic, rather than demonic. An archangel to protect the flow of time. Astonishing, really." Paul paused, thinking over his own research.

"I don't understand, Paul. How could this *thing* be an angel?" asked Ross.

"There are angels and demons that perform specific tasks for their masters. Somehow you triggered an event, got stuck in some sort of vortex, and ended up at this point in your past. You must be like a big, bright homing beacon to it, simply because you're not supposed to be here."

"But other people have seen it..." said Gary.

Paul nodded. "If this Griselphet is the same creature that has been seen over the years on the bridge, it's possible it has been waiting for the two of you. But why?"

They had no answer and he had no further knowledge to share. He handed the cross to Ross and wished the men good luck. With the talisman in their possession, Gary and Ross left and headed straight for the old truss bridge.

As they sped away, and feeling that their terrible ordeal was about to come to a head, Gary opened up to his son. "Ross, I know it's something I can't undo. But I realize now what an idiot I was for leaving you and your mom like that. I should've been there for you more over the years..."

Ross kept his gaze on the road. "What's done is done. I turned out okay."

Gary continued. "I know. I just want you to know that I'm sorry. I hope you can forgive me."

"It's not that easy, Dad."

"Son, I'm trying to…"

It was too much for Ross to process. The weight of his mother's death and the severity of their situation, the fear in his heart as he raced toward the bridge. "Stop, alright? Let's just get out of here and you can go back to Port Jervis and do whatever the hell it is you do."

Gary shifted in his seat and turned to Ross. "Give me a *chance*, Son."

Ross focused on the bridge ahead.

"I want to be part of your life now."

"You're thirty years too late. Mom's dead. I'm a *grown man*. Face it, Dad, you're nothing more than a bad memory at this point."

"Hey! I know you're upset about your mom. If you can believe it, I am too. And I get your anger—I really do—but you've got to give me another chance, Ross."

"You can't just show up and expect to patch things up in one afternoon."

"I'm not saying I can solve it in one afternoon, but we can start—"

"Holy shit!" Ross screamed and his eyes went wide. The opaque being was dead center on the bridge, blurring the road beyond.

Gary put his fatherly woes aside to tend to the matter at hand. He grabbed Paul's Coptic cross and held it out of the passenger side window. But when the car reached the being, both Gary and Ross winced—the hot, suffocating feeling returned.

Ross, unable to control his trembling body, turned the steering wheel hard to the right. His attempt to correct the vehicle's trajectory and slam on the brakes was futile, and the Prius slammed directly into the steel. There was a loud screeching, and the entirety of the bridge wavered and shook from the force of the collision.

A heavy blanket of smoke and dust hung in the air when Gary opened his eyes. He turned to his right and gasped when he saw Ross out cold in the driver's seat. Through the shattered front window, Gary could see flames rising from the hood. The old bridge creaked and groaned, the sound of rusted metal and rotten wood shifting.

"Ross! Wake up!"

The structure began to heave. Unable to stir his son, Gary threw open the passenger door, grabbed him under the shoulders and pulled him out of the car. He coughed as a cloud of dust engulfed them. Quickly, he carried Ross from the wreck and laid him down gently upon the asphalt yards away.

Gary shook Ross by the arms, screaming at him to wake up. A wave of relief passed over him when Ross opened his eyes moments later.

"Ross!"

Ross strained to speak. "Dad, what happened?"

Gary pointed back at the car and Ross lifted his head slightly to take in the magnitude of the wreck. The front end of the vehicle was smashed into the side of the bridge, the fender where the front seat used to be. Dark smoke billowed out as hot, orange flames raged on the hood.

"Did the cross work? Is it gone?"

"Son, I don't think—" Gary stiffened as he watched the opaque being rematerialize from a shimmering haze over the smoldering wreckage. As its massless form drifted toward them, Gary and Ross again felt the burning in their chests, the dizzying nausea.

The bridge began to wrench more insistently. Gary helped Ross to his feet and led him away from the otherworldly being.

"Mom's rosary," Ross said, just barely getting the words out.

Gary turned back toward the car. "I'll grab it; you just get off this bridge!" Ross watched over his shoulder as his father struggled against the heavy smoke and oppressive heat, soon disappearing from his view only yards away.

As Gary emerged through a parting in the wafting smoke, he caught a glimpse of the true nature of the being. The sun shone directly behind it as it hovered in the air. Its silhouette glimmered, revealing its human-like form and large, plunging wings. Gary's body was overcome by some form of current, deadening his movements. He fought against the being's projected power and trudged the final few yards toward the car.

Ross kept up his injured hobbling away from the accident and toward town, looking over his shoulder every so often to try and catch a glimpse of his father through the haze. He reached the road and anxiously waited there. When his dad finally emerged from the wreck, gasping for air, holding the rosary above his head triumphantly, Ross was overcome with emotion.

The bridge rumbled and groaned, its weight seeming to shift to one side. Gary sensed the impending danger and hurried toward Ross, but it was too late. The Depression-Era bridge had seen its last.

"Dad!"

The bridge finally succumbed to the havoc wreaked upon it. There was a cacophony of cracking and screeching as it swiftly collapsed, twisting into the creek below.

Ross cried out as a cloud of brown dust engulfed him and the surrounding area. Minutes passed before it had settled enough for him to make out the scene in the creek below. Somewhere among the wreckage lay his father.

Several townsfolk ran from nearby shops and buildings, staring in disbelief at the scene before them. Ross sat on the creek bank near the road, reeling. "Dad! Oh, God!"

As he stared at the fallen bridge, a man came up to him and asked if he was alright, and if he knew what had happened. Ross merely nodded, watching as emergency personnel showed up to survey the disaster. It was surreal seeing everyone clamoring

about, some of whom he recognized from childhood.

Ross was startled from his daze by a familiar
voice and a hand on his shoulder. "It's alright, son.
You're safe now. Just sit here a minute."

He looked up, shocked to see that it was his
father—the father from his past. Gary, the volunteer
firefighter, had heard the call on his CB radio, and
hadn't thought twice about responding to an
emergency before leaving town.

To Gary Everett's surprise, the young man
jumped up and buried his face in his shoulder.
Understanding that the man had undergone some
sort of serious trauma, Gary accepted the embrace.

"My dad..." repeated Ross. "He was on the
bridge."

"You're alright, son. You're safe now."

Ross looked into the eyes of the father from his
childhood, again wondering why he was leaving,
how the man's decision would weigh on him and his
younger self, the boy in the window, for the next 25
years—grateful that his final act was not self-
motivated, but dedicated to him.

He released his father and the world
transformed around him. The emergency workers
and the wreckage were gone. In place of the bridge
were a few stone pylons and a calm, murky creek.

Ross stood in the quiet stillness for some time,
watching the creek flow serenely around the existing
impediments. Eventually, a glint of sunlight caught
his eye, reflecting off something in the mud below.

He clambered down the embankment and out over the water, using jutting rocks as stepping stones. He again spied the reflected sunlight, and was able to find and retrieve the item. From the creek bed Ross pulled a golden crucifix, followed by its 59 red rosary beads.

A TALE OF PALPABLE VIOLENCE

Sherry straddled Bram in the backseat of her father's '82 Cadillac Coupe Deville, Bram's sweaty back sticking to the leather interior, as a Prince song played on the radio. The couple was riding high on a raw, uninhibited energy that summer night. They pawed at each other madly, soul kissing, as if they hadn't been in each other's constant company since graduation. Sherry's fingers slid down the foggy window, leaving five long streaks on the glass.

The song faded out as a deejay broke in with the top-of-the-hour news. The couple ignored it; they weren't about to let talk of the weather and spaghetti charity dinners get in the way of their fun.

A minute into his spiel, though, the deejay's voice grew grim and he uttered the words "masked killers," jolting the couple from their hazy reverie.

...Schuyler County Sheriff Buck Avery stated that police traded fire with the suspects earlier today, ending a week of silence from the perpetrators. Authorities had previously believed that The Cutthroat Clowns (known for their

distinctive rubber Halloween masks) left the state following their last violent outburst at a drive-in movie theater. The suspects managed to escape into the countryside during the battle with the sheriff's deputies.

State and local police are combing the area south of Odessa, where the killers were reportedly last spotted by a gas station attendant. With the gunmen at large, the sheriff has advised those in the area to stay inside and avoid the roads.

The station then cut to a previously recorded interview with the sheriff.

The perpetrators are extremely dangerous, seemingly targeting their victims at random. They have zero regard for human life and have left a long trail of dead to prove it. We are in pursuit of these heinous criminals and will apprehend them swiftly.

Sherry pulled Bram back toward her, but he resisted. "Christ, babe. Hold on. Didn't you just hear that?"

She nodded, then playfully tugged at his T-shirt. "So what?"

"You're not the least bit worried? Did you catch the part about them looking south of Odessa?"

The wicked look in her eyes faded to one of mild irritation. "I heard it, but I'm not scared."

Bram sat up and adjusted his shirt. "I think we should head back to your parents' place. I don't feel safe here."

Sherry leaned into the front seat and turned the radio off. She returned to her boyfriend and ran her hands over his chest and arms. "C'mon, Bram. Do you want to *fuck* me or not?"

But all of her prodding and cajoling weren't enough to get Bram's body to cooperate; his fear was too great for even her force of personality to overcome. Soon, she relented and they climbed back into the front seat. Bram pulled out and drove them down the country roads leading to her parents' farmstead.

After a few minutes travelling, a vehicle pulled up to within a few car lengths of the Cadillac, its high beams shining brightly in their rearview mirror. "What's up with this guy? I'm going ten over the speed limit," said Bram.

"He's just being a dick," said Sherry.

Bram drove on silently, trying to ignore the irritating light in his mirror. As they worked their way down the winding country road, the unknown vehicle periodically flashed its headlights off and on, as if signaling to them.

"What the hell does this guy want?!" said Bram, his voice trembling. He thought about what he had heard on the radio.

"He probably wants us to pull over so he can slice off our heads," said Sherry, grinning. Bram didn't laugh. "It's fine. Just pull over and we'll tell them to fuck off."

"Pull over?!"

Sherry grabbed his thigh and dug her sharp nails into his jeans. *"Pull over."*

"Okay, okay…" said Bram, grimacing from the pain. Sherry smirked.

He guided the car onto the dirt shoulder and the other vehicle stopped directly behind. Bram watched in the rearview as a figure got of the other car and headed toward his driver's-side window.

"He's dressed like a cop," said Bram. "Why didn't he turn his flashers on?"

"There are unmarked cars without flashers. My uncle was a detective and his car didn't have flashers," said Sherry, her voice devoid of its usual air of certainty.

The figure approached and knocked on Bram's window, shining a flashlight inside. Bram looked at Sherry apprehensively and rolled the window down a few inches.

"Where are you two headed?" asked the uniformed man.

"Sir, are you a cop?" asked Bram.

"Yes."

Sherry leaned over Bram and challenged the man. "Can we see your badge or something?"

The man retrieved his identification and placed it against the window. The words DEPUTY PRIVITERE were printed next to a plain photo of the man. "Where are you two headed?" he asked again.

"Deputy, you understand. There are killers out here shooting people up; and usually when a cop pulls you over it's with flashing lights and sirens," said Sherry. The deputy nodded. "Anyway, we're going to my daddy's house on Beardsley Hollow Road."

"I see." The deputy walked around the Cadillac, shining his light inside and around the vehicle. He stopped for a brief moment at the back of the car.

Bram looked nervously at his girlfriend, wondering what the cop was up to.

The deputy returned a half-minute later to Bram's cracked window. "You two go straight home and stay there. As you probably know, there are some sick people out tonight." He tipped his hat and returned to his car. The car peeled out, kicking up dirt and rocks from the dusty road.

"What the hell was that?" said Bram.

Sherry just shrugged and they drove back to her parents' house without incident.

They pulled into her long, forested driveway with their windows down and the radio off. All they could hear was the sound of the Cadillac's tires rolling over asphalt. Bram stopped the car in front of the detached garage.

Before getting out of the car, Sherry reached under her seat and tossed Bram an extra-large mask with purple hair. Then she donned her own, which featured bright-red pigtails and rosy cheeks.

Bram paused as she handed him a pistol she had stolen from her father's safe the week before. "Do we really have to kill your mom and dad, Sherry?"

"Of *fucking* course we do," she whispered in her usual scathing tone.

Bram shrugged and followed her toward the house. They were nearly to the front porch when all hell broke loose. Blinding lights flashed on and shone from every direction. A gruff male voice shouted out some kind of command, and a moment later gunfire erupted from multiple points of ambush, decimating Sherry and Bram. The couple had no time to process what had occurred as their bullet-ridden bodies crumpled together on the cold driveway.

An officer had to call a halt to the firing, as the men and women in uniform had continued to empty their magazines into the teenagers well past any point of reason.

"*Cease* your fuckin' fire!" exclaimed Sheriff Avery. "We got 'em!"

Several officers swarmed in and disarmed the deceased, handcuffing them out of habit.

"Goddamn, Privitere, are you gonna read them their rights now?!" asked Avery, laughing at the rookie. "You can probably see through them at this point." He walked over to where the young deputy was standing and placed his hand on the rookie's shoulder.

"You did the right thing, son. They would've executed you if you'd have given them the chance. These two right here are animals." Avery nudged Bram's corpse with his foot.

"Yes, sir. I just wasn't sure if they would really come back here, and I didn't want them to go off and kill any more innocent people," replied Privitere. He was still on edge from his solo pullover not a half hour before.

"You gotta take risks, kid. You spotted that purple clown hair under the seat. You took a risk and we got 'em, so don't worry about what *might've* or *could've* happened," replied Avery. "There's no time for second-guessing in our line of work." He spit on Sherry's masked face and walked off.

The other deputies and state police left their perches and hiding spots and gathered around. They congratulated the rookie cop, and each other, on a job well done.

At The Cemetery Gates: Year One

THE BURIAL VAULT

Tall oaks and elms loomed overhead, affording Tom and his friends just enough moonlight to maneuver the roots and loose rocks that lined the herd path leading from the cross country trails. They only carried one flashlight, which they kept dimmed, and took extra care to avoid rustling leaves or snapping fallen branches. Over the summer they had been caught leaving the woods by the school grounds crew, and had been warned about trespassing.

The group walked in silence until they reached the small, uneven hill on which the mausoleum stood. A sturdy, black iron fence delineated sacred ground from the forest at the front of the structure. At one time the fence may have served a more protective purpose, but erosion had slowly eaten away at the sides of the hill the vault was built into, and several large openings now rendered the barrier useless.

Despite its age and a lack of care, the granite structure was far from decrepit. An unknown family of good fortune had built a solid, long-lasting crypt, and it was nearly devoid of damage save for some wear brought about by tree roots and the harsh winters of upstate New York.

Tom smiled. It had been two months since his last trek to the vault. The oldest of the group, he had graduated high school that spring and had already started college. With a few days off for mid-semester break, he had taken the opportunity to visit his friends back home, who all still had another year at Tioga High.

"I know it's kind of morbid to say, but I really miss this place," said Tom, looking at the vault as if he was admiring his boyhood tree fort.

"You should come home *every* weekend; you're not even an hour away," said Mike, his best friend. "It's not the same without you here, man. What do they actually teach you in journalism school anyway?"

Tom laughed. "Ethics. And I have to admit, it's a lot more fun digging up ghost stories to tell you guys than it is to sit through lectures on AP style."

"Yeah, but you get to go to wild parties every weekend," said Dougie, the youngest of the group.

"Not *every* weekend," said Tom. "But it's definitely easier to get your hands on booze up there."

Sarah, Tom's ex-girlfriend, grinned. "Probably not this *cheap*." The petite redhead held up the group's entire supply for the night—a 12-pack of a thin, light beer to be shared among the five of them.

Ivan snatched a can from her and popped it open, taking a gulp. "Yeah, you're missing out on some real *fun*," he said. He was a newcomer to Tioga High but had already cemented his status as one of the "cool" kids, and was now dating Sarah. He grabbed her side possessively, pulling her toward him. Sarah pushed him away and looked at Tom uneasily.

Tom smiled at her sympathetically. He and Sarah had broken up before he left for school in early August. It wasn't so much that he was jealous, more so surprised that she was interested in someone like Ivan. The guy came across a little too egotistical, and he didn't seem that good-looking from Tom's perspective, either. Ivan was slight, pale, and could almost be described as "gaunt."

"So, Tom, how's Eric?" asked Mike as they ascended the final, steep slope.

"He's alright. I almost convinced him to try out for JV football, but he's more interested in astronomy and that kinda thing," said Tom about his younger brother. "He gets out, though. He likes to explore weird places like we did when we were his age. He's always sending me pictures of random abandoned buildings and junk he finds down by the river."

"You should bring him up here sometime," said Mike.

"Maybe," said Tom, who would, in fact, not even consider inviting Eric along. *He* could go out and party at a forgotten mausoleum in the woods, but he wasn't about to get his fifteen-year-old brother involved.

The group reached the vault door, which, due to settling and their repeated break-ins, was always open just a crack. A wet, earthy smell wafted out from the dark interior.

Mike turned to Tom and said, "You do the honors, buddy."

Tom grabbed the vault door with both hands and pulled back hard. The door made a cracking sound as it slowly inched open. When it offered enough clearance, Mike shone the flashlight into the doorway and everyone filed into the crypt. Tom shut the door behind them and Mike set the flashlight on a broken stone bench in the center of the room, pointing it toward the ceiling. It offered a weak circle of light in which they could commence their festivities.

The interior of the vault was in surprisingly good shape for its age. The walls were relatively smooth, and only a trace amount of dirt could be found along the floor. The granite tombs that lined each wall were covered with hefty rock slabs, which looked as if they'd been placed there only months before. It was more like someone's root cellar than a crumbling crypt, making it the perfect place to drink, smoke, and tell stories.

The names and dates on the door of the mausoleum had been worn away by time, but the relatively pristine markers inside the tomb were oddly marred, obscured, as to be illegible. The vault had been long-forgotten by the residents of Tioga, like so many other small cemeteries in the centuries-old hamlet. Tom and his friends had leafed through books on the town's history in the library, and had even questioned a local historian about the land, without divulging the location or existence of the vault itself. Still, the tomb's origin—who made the lonely mausoleum their final resting place—remained a mystery.

It was Ivan's turn to entertain the group, and he had promised to delve into the vault's legend. For the first few weeks he had only come as a guest, but this was the night he would have to prove himself, and earn full membership into the informal club. He had teased the story for a couple of weeks; his father had grown up in Tioga and knew some additional details about the vault, which he had promised he would divulge that night.

"You guys ever hear of the tin shop that used to be up on Halsey Valley Road?" asked Ivan, dropping his voice and affecting the timbre of some late-night monster movie host. Everyone shook their heads. "Well, there were a couple of rich families in town that owned a successful tin mill, one of which I'm related to. They did their best business in the 1800s. One of the owners had a son who was always making mischief around the fabricating shop, playing pranks on the workers, running around like he owned the place. Everyone hated him. He was a nuisance and a real liability.

"Late in the afternoon on a warm September day, there was a commotion in the shop; it turns out the tin stamp's big water wheel had jammed up.

When the bosses came down to investigate they found the boy lodged between a rock and the wheel, crushed and drowned. For years, there were whispers that someone had pushed him, but no one was ever arrested or charged with the boy's murder."

"Good riddance. Kid sounded like a little shit," said Dougie, cutting Ivan off.

Ivan paused and stared Dougie down before continuing the story. "The family was heartbroken. This kid was their golden boy and could do no wrong. They had the means and built *this very vault* in only a matter of days, to bury him." Ivan paused and looked around the room. Tom rolled his eyes at the theatrics.

"It was supposed to be a family vault, but the boy was the only one ever interred here. And I'm pretty sure they placed him *right over there.*" He pointed quickly toward the boy's supposed tomb, and everyone's eyes followed. Mike, who sat closest to the tomb, shuffled a few inches away.

"Why he was the only member of the family to ever be buried here was the *real* mystery. But you guys weren't the first to wander into this place. My dad and his friends used to come out here to drink and party, too. They couldn't figure out why this big vault was hidden away in the woods or why it had only one burial marker with a death date. They asked around, like you guys did, but no one had any idea— until they came across an old-timer who had heard the legend of the place. This guy was by no means old enough to have witnessed the events, but what he told my dad scared the hell out of him.

"It turns out the boy wasn't exactly *dead* when they entombed him. The townspeople started to believe that he was wandering out of the vault at night and killing their livestock, preying on small game. What kind of force possessed him, no one knew, but his nighttime activities were frightening the living. They found carcasses, mangled and lacerated, across town. One lady found her Labrador outside her house, completely drained of blood. They knew it was this kid because the vault door was found open every morning and there were fresh footprints coming and going from the hillside.

"After a particularly gruesome cattle mutilation, the boy's family set a night watch near the crypt to prove it wasn't their son doing these things. But the watchman attested, with great apprehension, that their son did, indeed, leave the vault that night—and he moved like an animal on the prowl. His parents set more guards the next night to try to keep him in his tomb. But it was no use. He savagely attacked them, and they all noted his unnatural strength. He nearly decapitated one of the men as he tried to run away.

"The next day the townspeople were in an uproar. They wanted to drag the corpse from the vault and burn it. The mother pleaded with her husband to prevent their son's desecration. So the father convinced his neighbors that he would barricade the crypt so well that it would remain sealed forever. He was true to his word, and his workers put in a long day closing up the vault to the outside world. The night killings did stop, but no one again set foot near the vault, and the mother and father carried a deep dread in their hearts and minds until death."

The group sat in silence, contemplating the nefarious history of the vault in which they were sitting. It was painfully quiet. More than one set of eyes wandered over to the boy's tomb. The tension in the room was cut when Dougie opened a can of beer, which he had been shaking covertly in the dark, and sprayed it all over his friends. Everyone started laughing, and the dark history of the vault became just another spook story.

Tom, who needed to leave early for school the next morning, said his goodbyes and exited the vault. When he reached the bottom of the hill, he looked back at the structure, curiously. Something about Ivan's story had unnerved him unlike any tale that had been told there before. He had questions about the legend and wanted to talk to Ivan's dad.

As he followed the path back through the woods alone, he considered similar tales of early burial and the undead. He jumped when he came across a dead rabbit on the side of the path. Its eyes had been ripped from its head, and half of its body had been torn open, revealing a small mess of organs and blood. Thinking back to the ghoul and the mutilations, Tom quickened his pace and hurried out of the woods.

When he arrived home, his brother greeted him at the front door. Tom wiped his boots on the doormat, plucking off a leaf and a small hunk of mud he had picked up on the way back. "Hey, Eric. What's up?"

"Not much. I've been touching up some of the photos I took at the old hospital last weekend." Eric was a budding photographer, who made regular outings around the county documenting some of Tioga's more peculiar landmarks. Like his older brother, he had a fascination for the macabre and paranormal.

Tom's eyes bulged at his reveal. "Dude, what did I tell you about going on private property?"

"It was only for a few minutes. I—"

"Stop. I don't want to hear it." Tom glared at his brother.

"What were *you* out doing?" asked Eric.

"I was over at Mike's. Sarah was there with her new boyfriend."

"Was he as big an asshole as I told you?"

"Just not the type of guy I ever imagined Sarah dating. Just weird. Where's he from?"

"I don't know."

"He said his dad grew up here. Wonder what made them come back to *Tioga*."

Eric shrugged.

"I just hope he's not a dick to Sarah."

"Next time let me come out maybe. I miss hanging out," said Eric.

"Sure, man," said Tom, humoring his brother.

Tom returned to college that Sunday afternoon. With a full course load, campus job, and regular outings with new friends, he didn't make any trips back home for weeks. He kept in touch with Eric, who sent him a series of photographs one weekend of a supposed UFO landing site in a neighboring town.

Tom was returning to his dorm from a party early one Sunday morning when he received a frantic phone call from Eric: "Tom, I don't know how to say this. It's so unreal. Oh, god..."

"What's wrong?! Is everything alright? Are Mom and Dad okay?"

"Mom and Dad are fine. Tom—your friends are missing. Mike, Sarah, Dougie. No one can find them. The cops are out looking. There were search parties out last night and everything. It's crazy."

"What?!" A series of blood-soaked images ran through Tom's brain. He pictured Sarah face down in the woods, her body blue and bruised.

"I don't know. They never came home."

Tom immediately rushed to his car and made the normally fifty-minute drive to Tioga in less than half an hour. All the way there, he thought of the vault. It was a weekly tradition, and he was sure his friends had gone there that Friday night to indulge in more horror stories and beer. But what happened? He thought of Ivan's tale of the tin mill ghoul again. The killings. The mutilations.

When he got to Tioga, Tom picked up Eric and they both headed out to the woods to meet up with the search party. Dozens of locals had joined the police. They wandered through the woods, calling out the names of local kids whose birthday parties they'd been to, football games they'd attended. Long beams of light cut through an early morning layer of fog. But all they illuminated were dying trees, wet orange leaves.

"Doug!"

"Mike!"

"Sarah!" Tom's voice broke as he called out her name. His throat felt raw.

Eric walked a few feet to Tom's right, doing his part. They had covered a large portion of the woods to the northwest of the high school when Tom realized that they were nearing the hill that led to the vault. When he saw that Eric was headed toward the hill, which concealed their unsanctioned hangout, Tom grabbed his brother by the jacket and pulled him in the opposite direction.

"What's up, man?" asked Eric.

"The cops already looked that way," said Tom. "C'mon."

They searched for another twenty minutes, their voices growing hoarse, bodies weak from lack of sleep, until they heard a man in the search party shout: "Oh, my god! Over here!"

Tom and Eric rushed frantically toward the sound, along with a few nearby members of the search party. When the two brothers arrived at the source of the screaming, they recognized their Uncle Phil as the man who had made the discovery. He had his back turned away from the scene and held his arms in front of his nephews.

"No, no, no, boys. Don't look. Just turn away," said Phil. But Tom, who had only the year before pledged his love to Sarah, ran around his uncle and saw the scene for himself.

The bloodshed was incomprehensible. His friends' remains were spread over a 20-yard radius, intestines and innards strewn over tree stumps and rocks. Mike's torso lay upon a bed of leaves, just a few yards from Dougie, whose throat was slit wide open. No part of Sarah's body was intact enough to prove her identity, but Tom recognized the butterfly necklace that he had given her on Valentine's Day.

Tom attempted to shield his brother from the carnage, but it was too late. Eric had already taken out his camera and snapped several photographs before their uncle smacked it out of his hands. The entire search party arrived soon after. By then the sun had risen enough to burn away the fog and reveal the full scope of the massacre.

Tom sat in his bedroom back at home, contemplating the last few days' events—Mike and Sarah's parents arriving at the scene; the harrowing screams; the funerals, where hundreds of Tioga citizens came out to pay their respects; the closed caskets. He told the police as much as he could. He didn't want to bring up their repeated illegal visits to the vault, for fear of arrest, but the sheer weight of the situation demanded that he come clean. He told them everything.

He was staring at an old picture of Mike and Sarah when Eric came into the room carrying a sandwich. "Mom said to give this to you. She said you have to eat *something*."

"Thanks," mumbled Tom. "Set it down."

Eric placed the sandwich on Tom's nightstand. Before leaving the room, he turned back and said: "You know, a lot of people think Ivan did it, since they never found his body or nothing."

Tom didn't respond.

"Don't you wonder what they were doing out there in the middle of the woods?" asked Eric.

Tom thought of the vault. Its heavy granite door. The musty odor. They were now nearly tactile memories. "Yeah, I wonder..."

A week later Tom returned to college. He found it difficult to concentrate during class, the images of his friends' bodies fresh on his mind.

His anxiety was at an all-time high when he received a new text from Eric. Attached was a series of photographs of a place Tom knew all too well. The sloping hill. The iron fence. That door that was never quite closed. And finally, a picture of the interior of the vault, which looked oddly disturbed and unlike the place where he and his friends had spent so many Friday nights. Hundreds of cracks had appeared in the walls and on the floor, as if decades of settling and decay had set upon the tomb overnight.

Accompanied with the photos was a message from Eric: "Check out this mausoleum I found out in the woods! It's awesome."

Tom frantically texted his brother back, warning him to get out of the area as fast as possible, wondering what person or thing could still be out there. When Eric didn't respond to his texts, then his phone calls, he ran out of his dorm, jumped into his car, and sped toward Tioga.

In the time it took Tom to reach the edge of the woods behind the sports fields at Tioga High, the late October sky had already started to turn a purplish hue. He hustled up the path, taking branches to the face and tripping over rocks. When he reached the hill leading to the vault, his chest clenched and he gasped.

Animal carcasses littered the path before him, their bodies cut open or mutilated in a way that seemed more a sinister game than the results of predation. Partway up the hill lay the body of a deer, its torso splayed open, blood still trickling out onto the cool grass.

Tom moved past the fawn and studied each new gruesome display. "Eric!" he screamed, his eyes fixed on the vault. "Where are you?!"

He had reached the top of the hill, but his brother was nowhere to be seen. As he drew closer to the fence, Tom noticed Eric's camera in the dirt. When he picked it up, he felt a sticky, slippery substance. He inhaled and his heart rate quickened at the metallic scent of blood.

Tom ran to the back side of the vault, but found nothing. He circled to the front again and stood at the door, staring at it anxiously before pulling it open and stepping inside. The tomb was dark and silent. Gone were the laughs, the smell of Sarah's perfume, the sour stench of beer, and in their place was an imposing dread. As in the photos, it now appeared more like the forgotten mausoleum that it was.

"Eric?" Tom whispered. He studied the tomb that supposedly housed the body of the boy from the tin mill. It was undisturbed, but no less unsettling.

He stood silently in the vault and listened. Nothing. He held up Eric's camera and started clicking through the gallery, wondering if he could glean any information from the photos contained within.

He flipped through a series of images of various landmarks and places of lore around the county—the satanic graffiti under the C.F. Johnson Bridge, the Helena Black tree up on Bowman Road, various graveyards—and came to the photos of the vault that Eric had sent him earlier. The date and time appeared at the corner of each photo. But there were additional images Eric had not sent. And they all bore the date of 10/14/16—the night his friends were killed.

Tom clicked through the remaining photos in the series. Another close-up of the vault door. A shot through the cracked entrance, his friends sitting inside watching an animated Sarah, likely telling a story. The next picture revealed his friends in shock as the cameraman entered the vault. Several blurry images followed, before the series ended.

He looked back through the photos in confusion. He was certain Eric had not known about the vault.

There was the sound of leaves crunching outside, and then a figure standing just outside the door. "How come you never invited me, bro? I like scary stories, too," said the familiar voice coming from the silhouette in the door frame.

"Eric?!"

Tom's little brother slowly walked into view, covered from head to toe in blood and fur. Tom shuddered and yowled in the agony that only a family member can feel when someone they love has done something horrific. Eric was holding Ivan's severed head under his arm like a football. In the scant moonlight that peeked through the vault door, Tom could still make out Ivan's distorted expression. Gone was the young man's cocky grin, and his eyes were completely devoid of their over-confident glint.

PASSION'S PAROXYSM

No *more regrets*, thought Ben Chapman as he sat aboard the northbound D train holding a bouquet of purple flowers wrapped in brown paper and covered in cellophane. The lengthy subway commute to his uptown apartment provided him an hour to contemplate life, and most of his thoughts of late had revolved around his wife, Judy.

As he looked at the bell-like, tubular flowers and admired their exotic beauty, he reflected on his marriage. The first year had been sublime; he and Judy had honeymooned in Spain, genuinely enjoyed each other's companionship at home, and made fervent love with an alarming regularity that was almost (but not quite) too much for Ben. The second year didn't live up to the first. He and Judy began to argue over money and future life goals and prospects, and soon discovered how little they actually had in common beyond superficialities: TV, music, movies, restaurants. It was a decent year, nonetheless; they moved into a larger apartment, took a short vacation, and were intimate at least once a week.

But a few months into their third year as the Chapmans, Ben's faith in his wife's fidelity began to waver. Judy would go out several times a week, for hours at a time, with no concrete explanation for her whereabouts. He worried that she was seeing another man, but was too afraid to confront her and make such a heavy accusation. After several weeks of excruciating anxiety, however, Judy's irregular routine became too much for him to brush off. He came home from work one afternoon and demanded that she tell him what she was up to.

"I've been going to a fitness center on the east side. I know it's kind of expensive, but I just want to look good for you," she told him, immediately breaking into tears in recognition of his waning conviction regarding her loyalty. "I wanted it to be a surprise."

Ben looked her up and down. It seemed feasible; she *had* lost a noticeable amount of weight. He apologized and brought her a bouquet of flowers the following day. From that point on, Judy was able to visit the gym anytime she liked, no questions asked.

Now, three months later, the train hit a rough stretch of track, causing Ben's entire car to vibrate and passengers to get shoved around. Ben made sure not to bump into anyone, as the flowers were extremely delicate. He was so excited to give them to Judy; she couldn't resist a fresh bouquet. He had even left work early so he could surprise her.

A strange-looking man mumbling to himself a few feet away grabbed a metal railing, and Ben instinctively reached into his coat pocket and grasped his folding pocket knife. This was no simple Swiss Army knife; it boasted a 3.5-inch stainless-steel, fine-edge blade and could do some *real* damage. When the train stopped shaking, the bum slumped down into a seat several feet away and Ben released his grip on the weapon.

The train soon arrived at Ben's stop. The doors slid open and he walked onto the platform and up the stairs. When he left the bedimmed confines of the subway terminal, the sun was still noticeably high in the sky, lighting up the ashen gray city streets. It was the first really beautiful spring day after a long, dull winter. He smiled as a warm breeze caressed his face. He hadn't felt so at peace in a long time.

He passed a woman talking loudly on her phone and it reminded him of another painful incident with Judy. Months before, she had begun receiving multiple calls a day, which she would always take into other rooms of their apartment. Again, Ben felt uneasy; his wife had never been shy about talking on the phone in front of him before, so why now? After days of this behavior, he had demanded to know who she was talking to. Again, she blubbered at his accusation. She revealed to Ben that her friend's husband was terminally ill and she was calling her up for emotional support. The next day, Ben had again come home with a bouquet of flowers. Judy inhaled their sweet scent and smiled, and all was resolved by the end of the evening. Judy continued to receive the calls without consequence.

Ben continued his walk home from the subway station, smiling as he passed a young couple holding hands. *What secrets do they keep from each other, blissfully unaware?*

As he crossed the street, he thought back to another episode from a few weeks earlier. Following an unexpected power outage at work, he had arrived home early to find a Corvette parked directly outside his building, jet-black with a noticeable scratch along the hood. He grew suspicious when the car seemed to speed off as soon as he approached, and had continued on inside the building, anxiously. When he entered his third-floor apartment and called out to Judy, she replied that she was in the bathroom and would be right out.

Ben went about his routine: removing his coat, pouring a glass of vodka, snacking on a danish, easing into the evening. When he tossed the remainder of his pastry into the garbage, however, he noticed a cigarette butt lying on top of a used coffee filter. Judy didn't smoke and neither did he.

When she came into the kitchen, Ben asked her who had been there and also mentioned the car outside. Judy initially told him nobody had visited, but Ben kept prodding; he wasn't going to let it go. Finally, after stumbling over her story, she admitted that Marco, an old college friend, had come over "for coffee, nothing more."

Ben felt he had been made a fool of. He stood silent, brooding.

"It's not like you think," said Judy, teary-eyed. "Just listen! My friendship with Marco means nothing compared to my love for you, Ben. I can't believe you think I would cheat on you! What kind of person do you think I am?!"

His wife having guilted him into rethinking his assumptions, Ben was forced to reassess the situation. *Maybe it was just an innocent cup of coffee,* he thought. *Maybe she's being honest. What proof do I have, really?"*

He apologized and told Judy it was fine to spend time with Marco, but that he preferred they meet at a coffee shop—not their home—from then on. Judy threw her arms around him and thanked him for understanding, and the two made love for the first time in months.

As he neared his apartment, Ben had a spring to his step. He had gone to a special flower dealer for this bouquet. It had to be extraordinary to make up for all Judy had done for him over the years. A bee flew through an opening in the cellophane and landed on one of the petals, and he smiled amusingly as it fell into the bouquet.

He was two blocks from his building when he caught sight of the same black Corvette which he had seen weeks prior. Rather than let it get to him, however, he continued toward his apartment. His days of suspicion were behind him. *No more regrets.*

As Ben walked into his building, he passed by a young, olive-skinned man in a leather jacket that made his own tweed suit coat seem almost grandfatherly. The man smiled at Ben, as if he knew him, and continued outside the apartment complex.

When Ben got inside, he removed his coat and set his pocket knife and wallet on the kitchen counter. He walked down the hallway and into the bedroom, where Judy was straightening the bed. She was startled when he entered the room.

"Ben! What are you doing home already?" Her hair was disheveled and the top button of her blouse was undone.

"I decided to leave work early because I just couldn't wait to see you, Jude." He held the bouquet out to her, carefully pulling away the brown paper and cellophane to reveal the rich violet flowers inside.

"Oh, Ben. They're beautiful," she said, taking the bouquet in her hands. She beamed at her husband and held the flowers up to her nose.

Ben watched as Judy's smile quickly faded and she started to hyperventilate. Her eyes widened and her heart began to beat at an unsustainable rate. She attempted to scream but could only get out a muffled and sickening croak, as her mouth had already filled with blood. Judy reached out for her husband, but Ben stepped back and let her collapse onto the hardwood floor. Her body twitched for several seconds before going completely still.

Ben thought back to his conversation with the botanist downtown just an hour before. "Foxglove is highly poisonous, sir. One whiff of these and you're out like that," the old man had said, snapping his fingers. "Be careful with these."

Stepping over his wife's corpse, Ben picked up her phone from the dresser and texted Marco.

"Hey. I had a great time today. Can you text me your address again? I want to send you something special!"

At The Cemetery Gates: Year One

THE HERMIT OF RUSSIAN LAKE

Big Moose Lake had been an out-of-the-way destination for vacationers and hunters since the late 19th century. It managed to retain much of its remote nature during the 20th century, unlike most of the Fulton Chain, a series of vast lakes not far south of Big Moose. While the other sizeable lakes in the central Adirondacks had become tourist hubs— lined with grand hotels, serviced by steamboats and railroads—Big Moose only begrudgingly built new settlements; and the hotels that did spring up were never all that successful.

Keith Lane had visited the area with friends over the years and wanted to share some of the charming solace of the lake with his wife, Becky, and their baby girl. He hoped to build a foundation for positive mutual memory there, and have a spot to return to each summer that they could make their own. He and Becky were having a difficult marriage, wanting different things in life, with disparate plans and goals. The vacation was meant to be a first step toward mending their relationship.

However, things never seemed to go as planned for Keith. Becky hated the cramped confines of the bungalow that her husband had rented. She complained from the minute they arrived, about the furniture, the lack of things to do, the difficulty of caring for their one-year-old daughter in an unfamiliar place. She really let Keith know that he was putting her out on this little vacation of his.

Not a day and a half had passed before Keith needed to get out of the cottage and away from his wife's niggling. Becky and the baby were sleeping, so he decided to take the canoe from the backyard and put it out onto the water. He knew from an earlier trip that in the eastern bay of the lake there was a dock, and from there a short hiking path to a campsite and pond. He was determined to ex-perience a little of his own type of vacation, whether Becky gave him a hard time about it or not.

The forty-minute-long paddle was leisurely, with a gentle wind at his back. Not many powered boats were out on the water that day, likely because it was overcast and threatening rain. He waved to a carpenter piloting a flat-top motor boat full of old dock lumber.

Keith arrived at the small dock and tied up his canoe. He found the marked, flat forest trail with ease and followed it toward Russian Lake. The path appeared well-travelled, and along the way he passed a man and a boy carrying a canoe, presumably back from the pond. They paused to talk.

"Hey. Were you guys camping?" asked Keith.

"Yep. We stayed overnight at the lean-to. It's really a nice, little lake up there," said the father. "It looks like it might rain, so we're trying to get back."

Keith left the pair behind and continued on the path for another half-mile until he reached the lean-to, which sat on a bluff overlooking the pond. He saw the obvious signs of the campsite in front: a fire pit, trampled grass, and indentations where gear had been parked for the night.

The pond itself held a small island, densely covered with trees, grass, and underbrush, as was most of the surrounding area. It was the end of the trail, and he thought it odd that there weren't more trails going off into the vast Pigeon Lake Wilderness Area which lay to the north, south, and east.

He wandered down to the small lake, peering into the brackish water for any sign of life. A beaver caught his attention as it swam from shore to the small island. He spotted the creature's bulky timber pile near a small outlet stream and searched out a spot where he could get a better look at the developing dam.

When Keith had walked far enough along the shore, he spied a gently tread game path that he could follow to the outlet. He waded through tall grass, flicking burrs and thorns, and swiped away various clinging bugs from his pants. Loons called out from a thick patch of reeds nearby; their eerie, almost wolf-like territorial posturing made him jump. Finally, he reached the outlet stream and looked over the beginnings of the dam.

The sun peeked out for a few minutes, and Keith saw something metallic shimmer downstream. He walked along the rocky brook toward the mysterious glistening beacon. Eventually, he could begin to make out some sort of structure among the trees. A little clearing had been made, on which sat a shack.

Keith had heard stories of the guides, mountain men, and hermits who had once occupied solitary settlements in the deep woods—men who had been present for nearly every exploration and discovery— the lore-makers themselves. He was a student of Adirondack history, yet was stunned at the existence of a hermitage in the 21st century—reasoning that the state of New York wouldn't stand for such a thing on its hallowed public land.

Smoke drifted from the makeshift chimney of the cobbled-together structure. The aluminum wall panels and asphalt shingle roof were set at odd angles—and the whole thing seemed about to collapse. Keith was startled from his structural study by the emergence of an old hermit, obviously the proprietor of this squatter's refuge.

"Are you lost?" asked the old man.

"No," replied Keith.

"Then get lost," said the old man, abruptly, and returned to his abode.

Keith paused, unsure if he shouldn't just turn around and hurry himself back to his canoe. The old man returned with a tobacco pipe in his mouth, already puffing at it in caricature of the classic Mountain Man.

"Sir, my name's Keith. I was checking out the beaver dam and saw the sun shine off the aluminum down here. I was just curious, you know?"

The old fellow sauntered over to him. They both stood about the same height, a little over six feet tall. "As you can probably figure out, I'm here on this land illegally, and any mention of my being here, to the wrong sort of people, will get me arrested and tossed out on my head."

"I won't say anything. I'm just at the lake for a week on vacation." Keith looked at the weathered shack and the surrounding area with curiosity. "How long have you been out here?"

"Decades… But who's counting?" The old man broke a yellow, wry smile, and continued to puff away at his pipe. "I suppose you'd like to see inside?"

Keith nodded and followed the old man into the shack. The first thing he noted were the modern provisions. There were canned food tins, a tidy collection of recyclables, and a newer portable propane stove. It all struck him as neatly utilitarian. The only non-essential items seemed to be a stack of hardcover books and a few magazines that sat on one small, homemade table.

"Do you want some coffee?" asked the old man, as he set some water to boil on his stove.

"Sure." Keith was directed to sit in one of the rough-hewn chairs.

"So, what do you think?"

"Sir, I'd have to say that I'm surprised at how well-organized everything seems."

The old man nodded. "Thanks. I've had time to get things right. Plenty of it."

"Do you hunt and fish for food?"

The old man looked at Keith queerly. "No. I buy my food in Eagle Bay at the market, the same as everyone else. I do make a little money trapping—legally, of course."

Keith was taken aback at how normal the hermit seemed. He figured there had to be something horribly awry in the psyche of someone brave enough to endure an Adirondack winter in such a hovel.

"Does it get boring out here?"

"No. Just simple."

"God, I wish *my* life would get simpler. I have a baby girl, and my wife is sure she wants us to get separated."

"Sorry to hear that, son."

"It's just so goddamn infuriating that she can upend my life because she's bored, or sick of it all, or whatever." Keith looked at the old man, who had been listening intently. He was embarrassed by what he had just revealed to the stranger.

The old man added some instant coffee to the now-boiling pot on the stove, and then poured two mugs, setting one in front of his guest. "You've a right to be angry."

"I'm sure life out here can be miserable and difficult, but it seems like it can be a paradise, too."

The old man didn't respond. He gave Keith a bagel and sat down in the other rickety chair across the small room. They sat in silence for a few minutes. Rain began pattering on the roof and aluminum walls.

"I should probably get back before it starts pouring," said Keith, standing.

"Do you have a motor?"

"No. Canoe."

"It's going to be a rough paddle back. The wind pushes east," said the old man, feeling briefly paternalistic toward Keith.

"I'll be fine."

"Don't exhaust yourself. Tie up to docks along the way and rest."

"Okay, thanks." Keith took a few steps to the door then paused. "You've got a real great spot out here. I won't tell anyone."

The old man nodded his thanks, and Keith left the cottage. He jogged back down the brook to the pond, then up to the trail that began at the lean-to. It was raining lightly by the time he got into his canoe on Big Moose. The water was already pushing roughly against the far eastern bank.

As soon as Keith nudged out onto the water he knew the wind was going to be a real problem. He tossed his backpack into the front of the canoe to try and keep the bow even with the stern. But his backpack wasn't heavy enough to keep the front end of the boat down, and the wind was pushing it each way, making paddling in a straight line impossible. He struggled against the piling water and strong gusts to drag the canoe, little by little, away from the dock.

The first twenty minutes were fine. He made decent headway and was practically within sight of a smaller bay to the south, which had a public boat launch. But the storm grew increasingly intense and he knew that he wasn't going to make it back to his cottage on the water. It wasn't a long walk from the launch to where he was staying, and he could return with his Jeep and grab the canoe from the parking area.

Twenty more minutes had passed by the time Keith realized he had gone no more than fifty yards. He was paddling furiously and his shoulders, back, and arms were fatigued. He knew he could always stop at one of the docks or even pull his canoe onto the shore and deal with the possibility of an unfriendly dock or cabin owner. A group of older ladies passed him with their speedboat and waved as he tried not to panic from his predicament.

The combination of a sudden blast of wind followed by a small wake from the passing boat knocked the paddle from Keith's hand. He lunged for it and had it nearly within his grasp when another strong gust sent him plunging into the water. The canoe tipped behind him, knocking him in the head. He struggled against his open life jacket in trying to find the surface, cursing himself for loosening it when he had begun to sweat from exertion.

The carpenter's flat-top boat, now devoid of cargo, pulled up alongside Keith as he was treading water. The man pulled him and his canoe on board. Keith, completely exhausted, could barely manage a thank-you to his rescuer. The rain was pouring as the boat cut through the choppy water and away from East Bay.

"Are you staying on the lake?"

Keith could only nod and point; he was out of breath, cold, and sodden. But he was able to direct the carpenter to the dock off the property where he was staying with little issue.

"Christ. Thank you so much, man," said Keith as the pair unloaded his canoe right onto the dock.

"No problem. You're not the first to get stuck out there. I don't know why they bother maintaining that dock and that trail to nowhere," said the carpenter.

Keith shrugged and tried not to grin as he thought of the old man. He thanked the carpenter again then returned to the cottage, unsure of how much of his tale he'd share with Becky.

* * *

The hermit of Russian Lake wasn't used to having visitors. Linear time for him was inconsequential, and how much of it passed between events was nebulous, at best. There were three seasons in his world and they merely cycled. Winter was an endurance event each and every year, followed by mud season (which coincided with an incessant black fly nuisance), and finally, summer.

Summer in the Adirondacks was the reason one would endure the other two seasons on the fringes of the wild. The hermit didn't consider himself 'of the wild,' as he benefited from modern convenience, the same as the campers who came out to his little lake every so often. He shopped once a month at the Big M grocery store in Eagle Bay; the hike wasn't bad at all once he found the maintained trails south of Big Moose.

He had enough money saved that he could continue his meager existence indefinitely. The Community Bank in Long Lake saw him once per year. He cashed his fur and hide checks, and withdrew a varying amount, usually based on the projected price of propane for the winter.

Though the hermit mostly kept to himself, a small legend had grown around his periodic appearances in the towns from Inlet to Long Lake. He had acquaintances that he spent time with during the hunting and trapping seasons. Most didn't know that he lived in the woods, and he shared very little of his past with them—a past which he had mostly suppressed, or nearly forgotten, by the time he had spent half of his life as a solitary recluse.

A young man appeared at his door one summer, as if he had been there before. He even seemed to knock as if he were visiting an old friend. It irritated the old man—the wandering curiosity of the upper-middle-class who descended upon the big lake from their luxurious 'cabins,' with party boats, speed boats, and now biplanes. They would traipse into his world from time to time, but they usually turned on their heels at the first sight of his camp, and well before making contact.

"Yes?" said the hermit, answering the knock, but not the door. He figured a little unpleasantness would be enough to send the visitor on his way.

"My name's Keith. I met you out here a few years back."

The old man shuffled to the door, exhausted from a morning spent chopping wood. He opened it but didn't recognize the interloper. "Yeah? I don't remember you."

The young man paused, considering if he should just leave. "I was staying on the lake with my wife and baby girl. I canoed over, followed the stream, and wandered into the clearing. We had coffee?"

The hermit looked at him quizzically, half-remembering some detail. "I don't get many visitors out here. And if I recall correctly, the last one may have drowned on his way back over Big Moose during the microburst. That storm did a helluva number on my cottage. It nearly tore my roof off." He pointed to some of the repairs he had done over the door.

"I'm looking for some advice. I think I might want to try and live a solitary life in the woods."

The old man chuckled, openly sneering. "My *advice*?! I'm the last person who should be doling out advice on how one should live."

"I'm not on a spiritual quest or something—I'm running from the police." Keith felt relieved to reveal his troubles to someone. "I'm just looking for a few tips, maybe an idea where I should go?"

The hermit's brow furrowed. "Are you a thief?"

Keith shook his head. "No. I just haven't been making the best decisions lately."

"No, you haven't. Someone certainly saw you come over here, and eventually I'll be found out because of it, and my home will be demolished. Not to mention, I'll be arrested like a common criminal." The old man looked the fugitive over. "Come in, I suppose."

He let Keith in and closed the door.

"Jesus. I'm sorry. She was gonna leave me. I actually saw red. I didn't think it was a real thing, but I actually saw red and the knife was right there on the cutting board..." said Keith, panicking.

"Stop it! I don't care what you've done or who you are. We're screwed now. Both of us."

Keith broke down, sobbing. "I loved her more than anything, and she just wrecked everything for us, for my daughter..."

The old man sat Keith in the rickety chair at his small wooden table. "Give me a minute. Let me think about this. We can figure something out."

There was a firm knock at the cottage door, and the hermit was pulled from his silent meditation. He nervously turned and approached the door, hesitant to pull the handle.

"Hello?" said a man's voice.

"Are you lost?"

"No."

The old man opened the door on a solitary hiker, a young man of about thirty.

"Sir, I'm sorry to bother you again. I was trying to paddle back out of the bay, but the wind was just too goddamn strong; so I turned back."

The hermit noticed that it was raining, the pitter-patter growing louder against his aluminum siding. "Again, huh? I'm really busy right now—just go back and wait in the lean-to for the storm to pass." He turned back to check on Keith, but he was gone. He looked around the small cottage for the man. "Keith?! Where the hell did you go?!"

The man at the door answered. "Sir, I'm right here... My name's Keith Lane, remember? We met and chatted a couple of hours ago. I'm vacationing with my wife and baby girl just down the lake."

At The Cemetery Gates: Year One

A LATE BLIGHT

"Dr. Stewart, there is a group of elderly subjects in Lestershire presenting with rapid lung and heart tissue necrosis, bulging facial tissue, swelling, cracking, and significant blood loss—internal and external," said Jesse Wright. "Early reports are pointing to a new variety of virulent sporing zygomycosis. I would like to assemble a team to retrieve and test soil and vegetation samples. Do you think you could recommend me for a grant?"

The tenured professor considered his student's request for less than a minute before turning him down. "Jesse, I understand you've done a great deal of work on this, but you're missing too much procedural information to present your thesis at even the most general level. There are just too many gaps in your data."

Jesse was crushed. He couldn't afford the equipment and team necessary to do anything but the most preliminary of tests. All he knew was that two elderly gentlemen and a woman had already passed away and others were sick, most likely due to this strange new illness.

"Professor, if I had a team, I believe I could pinpoint the fungi at the point of outbreak. It hasn't spread outside of a very narrow radius. There are maybe three suburban blocks exposed right now."

"Find the spores and run the tests; then we'll talk."

Jesse left his professor's office dejected. His own grandmother lived in Lestershire, the small, nearby town that was becoming infected, and he felt like he had plenty to offer in detecting whatever was causing the illness. All the medical professionals he had spoken to had more or less brushed off the idea that it was anything more than a particularly bad seasonal pin mold which would end with the first fall frost.

The following weekend, Jesse was staying at his grandmother's house. She lived a few blocks from the epicenter of the spreading sickness and he was determined to find the external cause of the malady, even if he had to search every plant and inch of soil in the neighborhood.

He sat with his grandmother at the dinner table, talking, mostly about the infection. "Grandma, where do you think the sickness is coming from?"

"Oh, I don't know, Jesse. Folks who've lived by that cemetery haven't had the best of luck over the years. My father never wanted to be buried there; he would always tell my mother we were too close to it already."

Jesse laughed at the superstitions of a bygone era. "What does the cemetery have to do with an airborne infection?"

She shrugged. "Mr. Miller and his wife were the first I knew to come down with it, and their property shares a fence with Valleyview. Mr. Donner over on Richard Street was always in his back garden just up the road from the Millers, and he was the third to pass from it. I know it's a nasty one, Jesse, because Mr. Donner and both Millers' caskets were closed at their wakes. It won't be long before it hits *this* neighborhood at the rate it's going."

Jesse noticed her tone waiver. He felt small in the scheme of things. As if a student could stop this undiagnosed, untreated epidemic.

Later that evening, he walked the streets where the disease had first emerged. Mr. Miller had lived in the same house since Jesse was a kid. It didn't seem entirely coincidental that two of the three streets with the most cases shared some relationship to the cemetery parcel. Richard Street was parallel and Wren ran to the northeast of Valleyview. The third cut to the east, perpendicular from Richard, which eventually intersected with his grandmother's road.

Jesse wandered through backyards, taking small samples of soil around dead foliage. He swabbed window sills on houses wherever he saw clumps of pollen, figuring the infection would follow a similar path on the wind.

It was beginning to get dark, and he was exhausted from gathering samples for his microscope, so he took a stroll through the cemetery for a look around. He was always a bit curious about the place, since his grandparents always seemed to lower their voices whenever they spoke of it.

Jesse remembered being a kid, sitting in the parlor watching TV, overhearing the adults tell tales about that old cemetery. He had played in the park just outside its gates all summer, and even ventured in now and then to see what the fuss was about. But it always seemed like an unremarkable place to him.

The graveyard was larger than he remembered. It didn't seem to have quite as many trees as it used to. Everything appeared neatly manicured, clean lines from weed whackers ran along the gravestones. Jesse ventured up the hill and mindlessly wandered off the path, under the cover of pines. He came upon more bushes, then older graves with stones faded into obscurity near the eastern fence.

Jesse passed behind an untrimmed hedgerow and saw an infestation of creeping vines covering everything from tree to grave to cemetery fence. "What do we have here?" Being a good scientist, he swabbed various parts of the vine and gathered a nice, complete specimen.

Jesse continued to study and retrieve specimens for days. He could identify every fungal body and spore he put under his microscope with the aid of his textbooks and manuals. He came across routine molds, some nastier varieties, although all entirely manageable. The creeping vine itself held no secrets, which was disheartening to a certain extent. He couldn't identify it, and a local florist and professional botanist couldn't identify it either. This might seem like a dead end, but for a scientist it meant that there was simply more work to do.

When school recommenced Jesse remained at his grandmother's, so he could continue his intensive search for answers. A man a few houses away seemed to be coming down with the infection, and Jesse was concerned for his grandmother's safety. They had long conversations about her life and the town's history each night after dinner. One particular night something she said resounded with him in a big way.

"Jesse, you can't imagine some of the things that have happened in this town, especially at night. Many horrible things—but not all bad. People say they've seen Indians walking from the forest down to the river when the moon is right and the seasons are changing. Something stirs up the spirit now and then, and it causes folks, the land, the air, to come alive."

The puzzle pieces were present in his mind, and he had been working on making them fit, but it wasn't until that moment that everything seemed to click into place. "It's been great talking, Grandma. I'm gonna be out late tonight. I think I have just the experiment in mind. A fresh perspective on our fungal issue." He kissed her on the cheek and ran to his room to gather supplies.

It was the dead of night when Jesse set up base in the dark, northeasterly corner of the cemetery. The gate had been locked. However, he had borrowed a ladder from a nearby backyard and made it over the fence with his gear. He managed to get the ladder through the fence, ready for a quick exit.

The late September air was brisk. Jesse was bundled in a hoodie and heavy vest. He directed his phosphorescent light at a mass of vines that crept along a series of small graves and sat down on a flat, raised marker. It was hard not to fall asleep in that soft, neon light, as he waited for a nighttime spore release. He took photos every so often of the lit area, but the vines' flowering mechanism seemed to remain inactive.

Finally, at around 3 a.m., as Jesse drifted in and out of sleep, he startled to see a mass entering the air around him. He snapped away, taking pictures of the floating, dust-like glimmer that was revealed by the special light. He tracked some of the spores to nearby flat, granite ledges and got his samples. Remembering his face mask, he quickly placed it over his mouth, in case he was right about this particular vine.

"Who's over there?"

Jesse's heart leapt at the sound of a gruff male voice somewhere off in the cemetery. Thinking it the caretaker having spotted his lamp, he turned the light off and gathered his equipment.

"What the hell are you doing out here?!" yelled the man, who sounded noticeably closer.

Jesse didn't wait for the man to reveal himself. He fled back to the ladder, tossing his possessions over the old iron fence. As he climbed the ladder he looked back over his shoulder, spying a tall man with a flashlight walking the easterly path. He thought he recognized the man, Mr. Lester, the cemetery's affluent owner, in the light of the moon.

"Get back here!" hollered Mr. Lester, shining his flashlight on Jesse as he made his escape.

Jesse scrambled over the fence. And as soon as his feet touched the ground he grabbed his equipment and sprinted back toward his grandmother's, unsure if Mr. Lester had gotten a good look at him.

Jesse was excited as his head hit his pillow that night. At the very least, if this vine was not related to the infections, he had pictures, samples to test, and evidence of what might be an undiscovered plant. Being able to describe and identify the first specimen of a known variety in a new region would be a great boon to his academic career.

The next morning, he spent hours in the lab at the university using the high-powered microscopes, which made identifying pollen, mold, and fungi a much easier task. The spores were similar to various known mucorales that had led to bleeding-lung deaths among children in Central America and rapid lung tissue necrosis in Eastern Europe. To him, it almost looked like a hybrid of a few incredibly virulent pathogens.

Jesse took his findings to Professor Stewart's office, but the man was out. He left a long note on the professor's door, describing how he had found an unidentified vine at a cemetery in Lestershire, with a new fungal pathogen that could be the origin of the spreading infection. He then went straight to the cemetery to speak to the Valleyview caretaker.

It wasn't long before he found the caretaker in his little shack. The older man listened keenly to everything Jesse had to say. "Sir, with all that I've told you about fungi, infections, and spores, I think the best course of action would be to cut down all of the vines and burn them."

The man, who had introduced himself as Jake, nodded at the biology student. "You're saying all of the older folks on Richard Street, and around the block, are getting sick from some plants over here in my cemetery?" He seemed open to what Jesse was saying, although obviously confused by the young man's technical language.

"I think if we get rid of those fungi-infested vines, your neighbors will start getting better."

"They are pretty unsightly. We kinda just let it be back there, since the graves are so old and it's out of the way. I'll talk to the owner, kid. Me and my assistant, Zeke, should be able to have them yanked and burned by this time next week."

Jesse thanked Jake, shaking his hand. Before he left, he reminded the caretaker to wear a mask whenever he dealt with the vines.

Not an hour had passed when Professor Stewart showed up at Jesse's grandmother's house. Jesse was surprised that the professor knew where she lived. They talked for hours and went over Jesse's findings in detail. The professor seemed very pleased with him.

"We'll have to fast-track your doctoral thesis. We could really use a guy like you at our research lab up in Geneva."

Jesse was flabbergasted at his professor's proposal. The research station was his dream job. Professor Stewart said he could get him set up by the following weekend, and that he would even let him stay at his second home in Geneva until he found himself an apartment.

The following Friday, Jesse said goodbye to his grandmother and headed up north to the research station, where he settled in quickly. Meanwhile, back in Lestershire, Jake prepared to eradicate the tangle of vines that had crept over the long-neglected grave rows near Valleyview Cemetery's eastern fence.

Mr. Lester and another man that Jake had seen in the cemetery from time to time came over as he suited up for his day's task.

"Jake, wait just a second…" said Mr. Lester, hustling over to the caretaker.

"Yes, sir?" replied Jake, pausing.

"I know we talked about clearing up the mess of vines up on the hill, but there's been a change of plans."

Jake was confused. "Sir, the kid from the college seemed pretty adamant that these vines had something to do with all the old folks in town getting sick."

The other man spoke up. "Hello, Jake. I'm Dr. Jim Stewart, professor of biology at the university. Jesse is a student of mine. I've seen all of his data, and there's absolutely no reason to fear these vines.

They're completely harmless. I heard about the small uproar he's caused, and came to apologize for him jumping the gun—coming out here and frightening you and Mr. Lester like that."

The caretaker looked at his boss and then at all of his gear, ready to go destroy the invasive vines.

"No, Jake. Don't worry about the vines today. In fact, you head home early and spend some time with your family. I'll lock the gate tonight."

Jake nodded and left, while Mr. Lester and Professor Stewart continued talking. "So, you're saying all this is being funded by the government, Jim?"

The professor nodded. "Imagine that. Uncle Sam runs some successful tests on a new biological weapon in a podunk town, and a cemetery owner gets bodies to put into the ground. How much are you charging these days for a hole six feet down, Lester?" The pair laughed grotesquely, as the fungal infection continued to spread throughout the blood, lungs, and tissue of Lestershire's oldest residents.

DELAYING DECAY

Like every other school-age kid in Lestershire, twin brothers Sean and Zack Grady were dreading the end of summer. It was Labor Day, and they had only a few more afternoons of freedom before their first day of the sixth grade. They had already spent their allowance and exhausted every possible avenue of fun at the carnival that weekend. Their parents' jobs demanded they work the holiday—Dad at the gas station, Mom at the laundromat—so the two brothers rambled around town, free to do as they pleased.

"Let's go to the comic shop," said Sean, the smaller of the two fraternal twins, as he and his brother strode down a quiet street on the town's south side, far from the annual parade that had just begun. They passed the empty husks of former shoe factories as they walked the weed-infested sidewalk.

"It's closed," said Zack.

Sean sighed. "What about the arcade?"

"Everything's closed. It's a holiday," said Zack as he and his brother crossed the train tracks that divided the north and south sides of town. Half of Lestershire was at the Labor Day Parade, which ran the length of Main Street, then passed down Memorial Drive, through working-class and white-collar neighborhoods alike. Thousands of citizens came out to watch the award-winning high school marching band and wave at local luminaries as they cruised by in floral-decorated floats.

"How come Mom and Dad have to work, then?" asked Sean.

Although Zack was the same age as Sean, he had taken on the role of an older brother. Sean had a learning disability and Zack often found himself in the role of protector of his undersized twin. Zack was already becoming aware of the social strata of Lestershire and his family's place in it. "Cause Mom and Dad have shitty jobs, that's why."

As they ventured further into the town's north side, the houses became larger, the lawns more thoughtfully manicured. They passed the hospital and the town's old high school and stopped outside of Coleman's Funeral Home. It was an attractive, well-kept building—a clean shade of white with blue shutters and doors with copper trim.

"They got real dead bodies in there?" asked Sean, his voice tinged with curiosity, and most certainly, fear.

Zack grinned. "Tons of them. They take them into the basement and suck all the blood out, inject them with a poison, and dress them up like dummies. It's so weird. I saw a reality show about it once."

"Sick! Why do they do that?"

"Preservation. It's all about appearances. Nobody wants to see their loved ones all pale and cut up. Or worse—decapitated!" Zack grabbed his brother by the neck and shook it playfully.

"Stop!" said Sean, pushing his brother away, chortling.

They continued down the walk and turned the corner at a row of tall hedges. When they came to the other side of the funeral home, neither of them could help but notice that the back door was wide open, the screen door gently tapping against the jamb in the late-summer breeze.

"How about we pay a visit?" said Zack, creeping around the hedgerow. "It's no arcade, but I'm sure it'd be interesting."

"Zack, no. What are you doing?"

"Don't be a pussy. Don't you want to see what they do with the bodies? The *freak show*?"

Sean shook his head. "Somebody's gonna see us."

"Everyone's at the parade, man. You think they're in there primping up bodies while everyone else is out having fun? They probably just stuff 'em into the freezer and turn up the chiller extra high for the day. C'mon." Zack laughed to himself.

Sean reluctantly followed Zack, scanning the area around the funeral home, making sure no one was watching.

They went up to the door and peeked through the screen. A long hallway with a rich navy-blue carpet and white satin curtains lay ahead. Several small lamps lined the wall, bathing the hallway in a soft yellow glow. There was no one around, no footsteps, voices, nor sounds of any kind.

"Let's go," whispered Zack. He slowly pulled open the screen and tiptoed into the hallway. Sean followed close behind.

As they wandered into the funeral parlor, they were surprised to find that it did not reek of rotting flesh, like some kids at school had said, but had a rather benign smell, something more akin to a church. The place was solemn but had an air of class about it.

At the end of the hallway was a long, rectangular room that contained rows of chairs. A lectern faced the chair audience, and beside the lectern, raised upon a decorative metal rack, lay an elegant closed casket.

"There it is!" Sean gasped.

"Shhh! Quiet!" Zack grabbed his brother by the arm and practically dragged him down the center aisle, pausing before the prayer bench. The twin boys crept onto and perched upon the bench, hovering over the dark mahogany casket lid.

"Does it just come open?" asked Sean, trembling.

"I'm not sure," replied Zack, feeling the smooth lid of the burial vessel.

They nervously felt around for a latch or grip to open the top portion of the lid. After some tinkering, Zack managed to pop it open an inch, pausing to take in his brother's expression.

"On three…" said Zack.

"One…" began Sean.

"Two… Three!" the boys said in unison. They flipped the lid open and revealed…an empty casket.

"Goddamnit!" exclaimed Zack, immediately cupping his own mouth at his outburst.

"It sure is a nice one, though," replied Sean, quietly content that corpses lay elsewhere. He leaned over the casket and fingered the silk interior and patted the velvet pillow. "This one must be for someone really rich."

Sean shuddered when he felt a hand on his shoulder abruptly shove him into the open casket, legs dangling over the side. "Ahhh!" He closed his eyes and grit his teeth, willing to accept whatever his punishment would be for trespassing.

He was relieved to hear Zack's loud, obnoxious guffaw in his ear. "Get the hell out of there, dummy." Zack pulled Sean from the casket and they got down off the prayer bench.

"Well, if anyone's here they definitely would've heard you scream like a little bitch, dude."

"Dick move, Zack…"

Zack slapped his brother on the shoulder and told him it was only a joke. "Come on, no one's here—let's have a look around."

The brothers wandered through another parlor, this one sans casket. They peeked into an office and a meeting room, then found the casket room, admiring the variety of coffin.

"What do you think these are for?" asked Sean as he knocked two metal urns together. The lid slipped off one and a small plume of dust wafted into the air.

"What are you doing?!" said Zack, giggling and coughing from the dust. "Those are urns. You just dumped a bit of someone's cremated body onto the rug."

Sean looked down at the streak of dust on the rug. He picked up the lid and gently placed it back on the urn before returning it to the shelf. "Gross. What'd it taste like?" asked Sean, looking at his brother, who was rubbing his mouth.

"Dirt," replied Zack, smirking. "Listen, let's get out of here. I don't think they have any bodies today."

The boys were about to return to the hallway when they heard the screen door open and close. "Shit! Someone's here!" whispered Zack. They hurried through a few different rooms and hallways, looking for a way out, or at least a good hiding place.

"Look!" said Zack, pointing to an open door. "Let's just go downstairs and wait for them to leave."

They hurried down into the basement and were surprised by the clinical nature of the room that they found. Gone were the warm lights and soft shades of blue of the first floor and in their place was a cold, white room, brightly lit, that looked like it belonged in a hospital. In the center of the room was a flat, metallic table, on which lay the body of an elderly woman dressed in a prim blue dress.

Zack quickly cupped his hand over Sean's mouth before he could scream. They both recognized the woman as Joy Petcosky, the mayor's wife. Her pale, expressionless face, bereft of its usual heavy layer of makeup, chilled the pair, as they were used to seeing her wide smile at town gatherings.

"Mrs. Petcosky is dead?!" whispered Zack, as he grasped his brother's shoulder for support.

Sean, in shock from their discovery, made to run back upstairs, but froze at the sound of heavy footsteps hitting the first few steps.

"Oh, shit!" Zack looked around the room and considered their predicament. He quickly yanked his brother over to a small alcove beneath the stairs. They crouched down behind a filing cabinet and a pair of red 55-gallon drums.

A man in a long, blue smock, whom they recognized as Mr. Coleman, hurried down the stairs and over to the metal table which held the woman. "Okay, Mrs. Petcosky, I've retrieved the correct-sized siphon pump, and we'll finish up here and have you ready to face your friends and family."

Zack and Sean watched with unsettling curiosity as the undertaker turned on the pump and attached it to a hose, which fed into a clear, glass cylinder. The machine broke the still quiet of the room with its heavy whirring. Sean gasped as the man unceremoniously plunged the pointed end of the tube into the side of Mrs. Petcosky's neck.

"Is he sucking out her blood?" whispered Sean.

"No, that's not blood. It's some sort of pink goo," replied Zack. The pump made such a racket that they had no trouble conversing in low whispers.

"Oh, nasty. It looks like her face is turning into a prune," said Sean. He laughed to himself as Zack grabbed his own mouth, gagging at the grotesque scene before them.

Mr. Coleman filled the cylinder with the pink sludge and poked and prodded at different veins and arteries of the old woman's body. Zack, transfixed by the scene, accidentally knocked a spigot from one of the concealing barrels. It clanked on the floor, causing the man to look up from his task. Both boys immediately ducked down as the Mr. Coleman turned the pump off. They crouched and listened for approaching footsteps, dreading their discovery. Eventually, after a few moments of nervous silence, they heard what sounded like the undertaker returning to his work.

The boys looked at each other, relieved that they hadn't been spotted, and again peered over the barrels. They watched Mr. Coleman remove the now full container and replace it with a cylinder filled with a dark fluid. Zack and Sean were speechless at the specter of the withered woman, who now looked utterly unfamiliar to their eyes. Her skin was taut to her skull and bones.

The man changed his latex gloves, placed a different hose on the new cylinder, and again jammed it into Mrs. Petcosky's neck. When he turned on the pump, however, something wasn't quite right. The crimson liquid began spurting out onto Mrs. Petcosky's face and even onto Mr. Coleman's mask and glasses. He rushed to correct his error, then wiped his brow, relieved to see the liquid returning to the body.

"My apologies, Mrs. Petcosky," said Mr. Coleman.

"Is that *blood?*" whispered Sean. "Aren't they supposed to be sucking it out and not putting it back in?"

"Yeah, that looks like blood," replied Zack. "This doesn't make sense."

Next Mr. Coleman pulled out a long, slim wire from a spool beside the table. He ran it through the woman's nose and throughout the different cavities of her face.

"I can't watch. Tell me when it's over," said Sean, nauseated. He covered his eyes and turned his head as Mrs. Petcosky's face contorted to the shape of the wire.

When Mr. Coleman had finished wiring the woman's face and pumping the red liquid back into her body, he cleaned up his work area and retrieved a mask connected to a gas tank. He straightened Mrs. Petcosky's blue dress, snapping various buttons back up, and placed the mask over her face. The undertaker then turned the release on the gas tank.

Zack nudged his brother. Sean reluctantly uncovered his face and watched Mr. Coleman pump Mrs. Petcosky full of some type of gas. When the corpse abruptly sat up both boys gasped. But the undertaker seemed not to hear, as he was busy trying to wrangle her body back down onto the table.

Zack covered Sean's mouth, as he knew his brother was about to scream. Sean bit down on his brother's hand as they watched Mr. Coleman restrain the elderly woman to the table.

"Mrs. Petcosky, your treatment is over. You are coming to," stated Mr. Coleman, calmly, to the flailing octogenarian.

Eventually the woman sat up of her own accord. The boys were astonished as they had witnessed Mrs. Petcosky go from pale and corpselike, to a withered, empty husk, and now she looked to be back to her normal, everyday self.

"What? But she was…" said Sean, trembling.

As if he were seeing out a client at a beauty salon, Mr. Coleman gave the old woman her heavy blazer and a hand mirror. She examined herself. "Well, I do feel much better now, Robert. Yesterday I looked like death itself."

"Yes, madam. I'm not just patting my own back," replied Mr. Coleman. "You already look twenty years younger."

"Hand me my pocketbook, Robert. I'll have to write you a check this month," said Mrs. Petcosky. She wrote in the amount of his exorbitant fee while he retrieved her shoes. "Are we still set for my special annual treatment next month, dear?"

"Yes, ma'am. I will receive my Guatemalan shipment mid-month."

Mrs. Petcosky stood with assistance from Mr. Coleman, still wobbly from the aftereffects of her treatment. "Robert, how often have you been seeing Julia Wheeler? She has been looking more supple than normal. You aren't giving her *my* special treatment, are you?"

Mr. Coleman smirked. "Oh, no, no, Mrs. Petcosky. You are my best client and my first priority."

"I'm sure, Robert. Thank you very much." The undertaker assisted the old woman to the stairs and past the hidden twin boys.

"There are so many new advancements in mortuary science, but we here at Coleman Funerary Services are on the cutting edge," stated Mr. Coleman as they walked up the stairs. "It *is* a very experimental science, and therefore expensive—but we feel that serving the mayor's wife, giving her the best treatments we have to offer—is very much our civic duty."

Zack and Sean heard the door close and listened for the footsteps to fade into another part of the house before they came out from their hiding spot.

"What the *hell* was that?!" exclaimed Sean.

Zack shrugged. "Let's get out of here while he's taking her to her car."

The pair crept up the stairs, listening for footsteps. "You think what they're doing is illegal, Zack?"

"Probably. Sounds like an underground, black market type of thing."

When they reached the landing they slowly opened the door. Seeing the hallway was clear, they hurried toward the rear of the house. Zack threw open the screen door and the brothers made a run for it.

"Ahhhh!" The boys screamed as Mr. Coleman stepped in front of them, blocking their escape, grasping both by the shoulder. They tried to shake free from the imposing man's grip, but he held tight.

"Boys, boys, boys. Hold on a minute," said Mr. Coleman, letting up as the boys ceased struggling. "Did you find what you were looking for?"

"Wh-wh-what do you mean, sir?" asked Zack, trembling.

"Trying to catch a glimpse of the recently deceased? You're not the first kids to sneak around my funeral parlor, peeking under coffin lids."

The boys looked at each other, sure that they hadn't been spotted during their upstairs exploration.

"We're sorry, sir. Please don't tell our parents," said Zack, relieved that the undertaker had not seemed to notice their basement voyeurism.

"Oh, I won't," replied the man, reaching into his pocket, as the boys shied away. "Hey, aren't you Ethel Grady's grandsons?"

Sean nodded meekly.

Mr. Coleman removed a business card and handed it to Zack. "You just give your grandmother this card and have her call me. And we'll forget about your little intrusion."

Zack pocketed the business card as the man stepped away, and the boys instinctively ran. As they headed for the safety of home, they passed by dozens of familiar faces leaving the parade and wondered how many more of Lestershire's elite were partaking in Coleman Funeral Home's special treatments.

THE GIRL WITH THE CROOKED TOOTH

In homage to Edgar Allan Poe on his birthday

In Human Anatomy and Physiology this pretty girl with a peculiar nose used to tell me she didn't want to graduate. I don't think I got more than a B or B-minus in that class, and I'm sure she made straight A's. I spent too much of my time studying the peculiar nose on this girl's face to get straight A's in anything.

To begin at the beginning. If the right eye-tooth is the same as the right lateral incisor, I'd be surprised, since I wasted so much of my time fantasizing. See, there was this pretty girl with a peculiar nose, you see? And I don't remember her name, but she wasn't you. And this note is about you and your crooked tooth.

A-ha! You'd hate that I mentioned your crooked tooth in some little confession or love note I'd written you. Now, if we were to meet today, would you still let me tickle your tongue and teeth with mine? I'd still know the space that deviates. I'd know it by day-dream and in dream-sleep. It's a little to the left and it turns in, the tiniest concave spade.

You hide it when you laugh, sometimes when you smile. And it's a sin how you'd hide anything from me. "That all your teeth were ideas" and you wouldn't share a thought with me. When every step I take is in dedication of you and all your perfect imperfections.

But now you're likely aghast, and your misery made manifold. I apologize. I should have censored myself from the intimate description. It's my training in anatomy, the attention to detail that makes me a bit blunt regarding the bits and pieces that deviate from the norm. When I come upon cadavers, I can't help but regard their symmetry and remark on any inconsistency in my notes.

You mustn't be jealous and bring her up again. She was just a girl to me; that posh girl with the peculiar nose. You were my first woman, and *oh*, were you a specimen!

To think in some dental office somewhere lay x-rays of your brilliant smile. The sublime 29, two that never surfaced, and the one that is uniquely you. I still can't believe how upset your parents became when I asked for a copy of your last dental x-ray. I'll send them a fruit basket with my sincerest apologies. I assumed that your mother would have kept it in a filing cabinet with all her notes about you. The pictures you drew as a young girl in Greene, your accomplishments, report cards, life insurance forms, etc.

Please don't be upset that I've written notes on you. It's only for my own perusal, for my art. That I may represent my muse in all her glory, in full regalia of our native tongue. Oh, your tongue! Your lips! Your mouth! How I would sit and watch you patiently, for your mouth to divide and reveal yourself to me. Even when I knew you were bored by my presence, I would hang on every parting of your lips.

How time passes swiftly. It was only time I desired. To be in your presence. But now they're here, and they've come for my notes and my labors. You will remain as you are to me, always. Like your eyes, my memory of you will never age. Your final gift to me I will not abdicate to the uncouth and unlearned of this world. That tiny imperfection that you gifted to me upon parting. A tooth for a tooth. Most artists say a muse is made to suffer. But my pain is trivial when I tickle our right lateral incisor in memory of you.

NEW YEAR'S EVE, WHAT A GAS!

James and Claire Ward were only hours away from
heading out into the revelry of New Year's Eve,
frantically searching for the right clothes, shoes, and
jewelry for one of the most exciting nights of the
year. Claire was digging through a box in her
bedroom closet, looking for some of her great-
grandmother's antique jewelry, which had recently
been passed down to her after her mother's death.

"Why are you rummaging through that old
box?" asked James, as he dug through his dresser
trying to locate a very specific cologne. "We've got
to get a move on it."

"I want to find this turquoise necklace my mom
used to wear during the holidays," said Claire. "It
was my German great-grandmother's. Plus, it's
fabulous and would match my dress perfectly."

Claire moved aside a few unremarkable items
until she came upon something that caught her eye.
"Oh, what's this?" she said, as she pulled out a
musty, old journal with a decimated cover and bind-
ing. She flipped through the brittle pages. "Gosh,

James, I think this is one of my great-grandma's cookbooks."

James came over and examined the book himself. The writing was small and in German.

"Can you read any of this?" asked James.

"I think so; my German isn't terrible," replied Claire, giddily. "My grandma taught me the basics." Her eyes scanned the pages and a smile crossed her face. "Think of how cool it would be if we showed up to the party with an authentic German dish?"

"We only have a couple hours. You'll probably have to go to the store to pick up some ingredients, and who knows how long it'll take to prepare," said James, cautiously, knowing his wife had no cooking ability whatsoever not wanting her to get frustrated.

"I'll find something simple," said Claire. She flipped through the pages for a few minutes, as James sought out the right tie for the night. "Here we go. This is all stuff we should already have. Ooh, it looks like a savory sauce. I have those brats in the freezer, James. I'll prepare the sauce, fry the brats, toss it in a ceramic dish in the oven. Should be ready to go in an hour or so."

"That's fine, Claire, but how will you have enough time to do that and also get ready? It practically takes more time than we have now..." said James, but he was cut off by his wife.

"Don't you dare finish that thought, Love." Claire whisked away to the kitchen, cookbook in hand, to begin her preparations.

An hour or so later, James was sitting on the sofa drinking a glass of brandy while Claire finished dressing. She came downstairs to a whistle from her husband. She looked great, and she was wearing her great-grandmother's necklace.

"Honey, could you please get the brats out of the oven and cover them while I get my heels on?" asked Claire.

"Sure thing, baby. And I have to say, you are looking fine tonight," said James, grinning.

The couple scurried about the house. It was already 10:30, and it would take them fifteen minutes to get to the party.

"God, that sauce is something *potent*. It made my eyes water when I opened the oven to cover it," said James as he emerged into the living room, coat on and ceramic dish in hand.

"I added a little extra horseradish to it," replied Claire, as they fled out into the chilly, late-December night.

They arrived soon after at the Grignard's. The party was alive, boisterous. Champagne and beer flowed freely as the Wards made their way through the living room, greeting friend, acquaintance, and stranger alike.

"Claire, what do you have there?!" exclaimed a tipsy Victoria Grignard, the lady of the household. She took the brats from Claire and dashed off to the kitchen without waiting for a response.

James and Claire were soon sipping champagne and sampling shrimp and finger foods from long tables in the dining room. They drank, danced, and schmoozed with many old friends as the clock approached midnight.

It was ten minutes before the new year when the partiers heard horrific screams from Victoria and two other women in the kitchen. Several men rushed into the room, toward the agonized howls, only to retreat—coughing, hacking, and dry heaving.

The gas coming from the kitchen was palpable. As James and Claire stampeded toward the front door in a haze, following the other terrorized guests, they turned back to see Victoria stumbling out of the kitchen. Her face was covered in putrid, red spots, and her eyes were turned up into her head. Blood gushed from her nose onto her plush, white carpet, which she fell onto seconds later, wailing.

James and Claire both felt the gentle burning in their lungs long after they had made it out of the house. They were sitting on the grass with their friends, choking and vomiting from the foul air. Emergency service personnel were soon on scene, triaging gassed men and women, taking many away in ambulances.

"What happened? Does anyone know what happened?!" cried a tearful Claire to a group of hacking firefighters, who had pulled a lifeless Victoria from the house only minutes prior.

"Some sort of poison gas, ma'am," replied the fire captain as he bent over and vomited on the lawn.

"Oh, my god, from where?!" shrieked Claire. James attempted to settle her so the firefighters could return to their work.

Soon after, James and Claire were cleared to go home by the paramedics. The couple began 2016 in abject misery and poor health.

The following week, after Victoria Grignard's funeral, the Wards were visited by two detectives from the local precinct.

"Homeland Security thinks this was a case of domestic terrorism, Mr. and Mrs. Ward," said Detective Ford. "We're taking it very seriously."

"Terrorism? Oh, my god!" exclaimed Claire. "At the *Grignard's*?!"

"Yes. Someone brought a white, ceramic dish to the party, containing what appears to be the chemical compound dichlorodiethyl sulfide—more commonly known as mustard gas," replied the detective.

"Mustard gas?!" yelled a confused James.

"We've now interviewed everyone at the party and no one seems to recall who brought the dish," said Detective Ford as he and his partner headed toward the door. "Take my card and call me if you remember anything else about that night—anything suspicious or anyone that may have held ill will toward the Grignards."

The couple nodded, shaking from the revelation, not revealing their ownership of the dish out of unmitigated fear. When the detectives pulled out of the driveway, James and Claire raced upstairs, threw open the bedroom closet, and pulled out the box that contained the cookbook.

"What the *hell* did you make, Claire?!"

She flipped through the book while James searched the box for any clue of what went wrong.

"Was this your great-grandfather?" asked James as he held up an old, faded picture which was attached to some German army papers.

"Yes. I think his name was Fritz. He won the Nobel Prize," replied Claire, matter-of-factly, looking over the photo and the papers, then returning to the tattered book.

"Fritz *Haber*!?" screamed James. "Claire, I've seen entire programs about him on the History and Science Channel. He designed the chemical warfare program for Germany during World War I."

Claire was speechless. James grabbed the book from her, and asked her to point out the page with the recipe she had used. He made her translate every ingredient. His mouth opened in terror as he realized that she had made a savory sauce using household chemicals. It wasn't her great-grandmother's cookbook; it was a chemist's journal!

"Oh, my god, James. I gassed our friends!"

"Claire, how could you know so little about cooking that you'd put ammonia or bleach in food?!"

"James, I'm a tenured gender studies professor, not the head of Le Cordon Bleu Culinary School!"

Tears ran down Claire's face. She and her husband fell silent, staring at the journal, wondering how long it would be before the detective and his men came knocking at the door again.

THE CALL IS COMING FROM INSIDE THE HOUSE

The Colonel's Library, November 1998

The Colonel sat in his vast library with an ancient parchment in hand. He had spent years, decades even, and countless dollars in search of the scroll. The thousand-year-old ink, only mildly faded, intricately spelled out before his ravenous eyes: *Grimoire Scroll of Berossus as Translated by Adelard of Bath.*

He had invested innumerable hours studying the scroll, obsessively cross-referencing what he had previously read in a later fragmented translation available on the Internet. The Colonel was certainly neglecting his wife Melinda and his daughter Heloise in the process, but he was not one to worry long over the dejection of others.

Clack, clack, clack. Someone was knocking at the front door. *Likely Brother Joseph looking for his monthly tithe*, he thought. A minute later he heard footsteps coming down the hall and two light taps at the library door.

"Come in," he sighed. To his surprise, his old friend Dr. Travis appeared.

"Who's the new girl?" said Travis.

"Heloise's babysitter."

Travis smiled peculiarly and nodded. "How's business, Colonel?" The doctor sat across the study table from the Colonel and took in all of the ancient books, scrolls and manuscripts his old friend had collected. Bookcases took up every inch of wall space, and the Colonel had piles of musty texts before him.

"I consider myself retired from the trade, Travis," said the Colonel. "The munitions and armament business has remained in a decades-long trough since the treaties were signed." In truth, the Colonel had been removed from the board of directors of the company he had founded and his financial situation was quickly becoming dire.

"So, doctor, how is my wife's therapy coming along?" asked the Colonel, moving on from the uncomfortable topic of his financial failings. Melinda had been seeing Travis, a professional psychiatrist, for months, and the Colonel had noticed a remarkable improvement in her day-to-day demeanor.

"Very good, sir. We've been combing through many of her painful memories from childhood and she's dealt with it all admirably. The future of her treatment is actually the reason why I stopped by today," said Travis.

"That's my girl," replied the Colonel, not letting the doctor finish his thought about the future of his wife's psychiatric counseling. The Colonel rambled on about the direction of the state and the misguided senators' dealings with unscrupulous politicians.

Dr. Travis noticed the scroll in front of the Colonel and recognized its author. "Have you finally acquired Berossus' spell book?" The Colonel nodded. Travis had a keen interest in the occult, but was a novice in the lore compared to the older gentleman.

"It's complete, Travis. I've nearly made it through Bel's Resurrection," the Colonel remarked, excited by the task at hand.

"Is the Prophecy intact?" asked the doctor.

"Yes—and by my latest calculations, Tiamat should soon rise and Bel will return to begin the Final Epoch," said the Colonel, nearly giddy in anticipation of the end of the current order. He had come to attain a doctoral-level proficiency in astronomy during his study of the Mesopotamian histories and lore books. His observatory on the property boasted the latest lens technology.

The Colonel showed Travis some of the text and macabre artwork that decorated the scroll. Demonic forms and depictions of warring pre-biblical gods sat in the margins. Odd skulls and even human autopsies were intricately detailed alongside spells and enchantments for raising the dead.

Dr. Travis was mesmerized by the pictorials, diagrams, and what he could glimpse of the enchantments. The Colonel was greedy with his life's work and soon moved the manuscript away from Travis' prying eyes. He had spent a small fortune and invested so much of his own blood, sweat, and tears in acquiring it that he felt Travis unworthy of the special knowledge it contained. A knowledge he was already putting to use, setting the wheels in motion toward regaining his once great wealth and political clout.

"Yes, of course—now the reason for my being here. I came to deliver this letter to Melinda, regarding her treatment. I think we've come as far as we're going to go together," said Travis.

The Colonel accepted the letter without question and wished his friend well. He immediately returned his attention to the ancient scroll on the table.

Melinda's Bower

Melinda sat in silence in her third-floor room with the sealed letter from her psychiatrist. The Colonel referred to this personal space of hers as 'Melinda's Bower.' The large Victorian mansion had many rooms that the Colonel adored—his library, the wine room, observatory—but Melinda herself only cared for her comfortable boudoir.

She opened the envelope with a penknife and nervously removed the letter from her lover.

Dearest Melinda,

I don't regret what we began or what we have come to be. I was never in a position to analyze, diagnose, or treat your gift. It truly was a gift in your youth, and remains so. You have come into a knowledge that far surpasses anything in the ancient manuscripts your husband hoards in his library.

My wife is my partner in this world. What you and I shared was otherworldly. I won't be so callous to say that we part as friends, but we must be parted for the sake and friendship of each party. I know in my heart that we will be joined again when the Prophecy resolves.

Your part in the resolution of this world has yet to be written. Dreams and visions are only as premonitory as a synchronous series of events can be predicted or premeditated.

Ever Yours,
H. P. Travis

Melinda wept into the brief, yet poignant, note from the doctor. She was at odds with the puzzle of her ability expressed as a 'gift', yet moved by the professionally unemotional doctor's clear expression of undying affection toward her.

She knew the Colonel could never feel or express what she and the good doctor had shared during those sessions. Now she had no more visits to look forward to, no more anxiety filled hours in anticipation of the conversations she and Dr. Travis would have, they places they would visit. Before her she faced only a bitter disallowance.

Melinda knew her living hours from then on would be unbearable, unthinkable. Heloise would be well cared for. Her family was wealthy, and independent of the Colonel's failed contracts and money-grubbing war machinations.

Later that night, in her third-floor bower, Melinda separated herself from her material relationships at the end of a hanging rope.

A Colonel's Tithe

A young redhead, not quite twenty, answered the door and let Brother Joseph in. He was rector of the local seminary school and well-known among the townsfolk as a lascivious Franciscan.

"*Well, hello*, miss. Is the Colonel home?" asked the monk.

"Yes, Brother. He's in his study. But he asked to not be disturbed," replied Jordan, young Heloise's beloved babysitter.

"We're old friends; I'm sure he won't mind, dear," said Brother Joseph, eyeing the teen girl in a wholly inappropriate way as he passed to the staircase and up to the second floor of the home.

The Colonel heard the overweight monk in the hallway outside of the library and sighed in disgust. He had been practicing newly discovered ritual spells and hexes, searching for the correct pronunciation of Latinized words he had never seen before.

"Come in, Brother Joseph," called out the Colonel, before the Franciscan had a chance to knock.

The monk approached the table and noticed that the Colonel was studying a statue of what appeared to be an Egyptian pharaoh fighting an English griffin. He then read a partial Latin script on an old manuscript beneath the artifact—"*ad bellum facere proximo*"—*which* he was able to loosely translate as "*the next (or final) war.*"

"This is very interesting, sir," said Joseph as he tried to get a better angle on the text in front of the Colonel.

"It's just a little history study, Brother. Your check is in my office," said the Colonel as he closed the spell book before the well-read eyes of the multilingual educator.

"This statue, is it Assyrian?" asked Brother Joseph.

"No, Babylonian," the Colonel replied. He was getting anxious over the monk's budding interest.

"How about a drink, Brother?"

Brother Joseph smiled as the Colonel got up and led him to his wine room just down the hall. It had become their monthly ritual. The monk collected the Colonel's tithe for the school and they would share a bottle of fine wine from the Colonel's collection.

The Colonel poured two glasses of an old French vintage in the wine room. Bottles lined the walls, corks directed toward the center, nestled in antique wooden racks.

"You have most excellent taste, as always, Colonel," said Joseph. The Colonel nodded.

"The Anglicized Latin, I know it very well. Adelard, Friend of the Orient. You can never be too careful when wading into Near East mysticism," warned Joseph.

The Colonel didn't respond, knowing who paid for the nice clothes and cars that the school clergy enjoyed, and he finished his glass.

The silence of the room was disturbed by a cork popping and some liquid pouring forth, landing mere feet from the expensive shoes of the two men.

"What in the..." the Colonel began, before being startled by more corks popping and a dark red liquid streaming from individual bottles onto the floor, walls, and shoes of the pair. The two men shuffled about, attempting to get to the door and also to avoid the sanguinary eruptions.

"This isn't wine!" exclaimed Brother Joseph.

Their clothes were stained a blood red by the time they emerged into the hallway. Before they had time to catch their breaths from the shock of the wine room, they heard a woman screaming, seemingly from the third floor.

The portly monk struggled to keep up with the Colonel, down the hallway and up the stairs to Melinda's room. They discovered the source of the shrieking—the babysitter—and the reason for her cries. The Colonel's wife, Melinda, hung from a rope above her settee.

"As I was putting Heloise to bed, I heard a thump above us, so I came up to check on Melinda," said Jordan, openly weeping from the trauma of her discovery.

The men saw to Melinda as the babysitter returned to the nursery with Melinda's from Dr. Travis tucked in her back pocket.

The Babysitter

Jordan chased Heloise through the foyer as Melinda lay on a table in the ballroom, wrapped in a winding sheet. The Colonel had left her and the toddler in the mansion while he went to the police station to answer questions about his wife's sudden death.

The phone rang, and Jordan went into the kitchen to answer it.

"Hello?" No response.

She hung up the phone and returned to her charge. Minutes later, the phone rang again and she returned to the kitchen, but this time she let it buzz a few times. She noticed that when the antique bell paused, she could catch the tail end of the ringer from the phone in the Colonel's office on the second floor.

"Hello?"

"Get out of the house!" commanded a man's muffled voice.

"Who is this?" asked the babysitter.

The man hung up. Jordan was frightened by the warning, but didn't know what to do, as the Colonel was supposed to return any minute. When the phone rang again she answered it quickly, demanding to know who was calling.

"She was sacrificed," said the stranger on the other end of the line.

"Who are you?! This isn't a game," she shouted, angrily.

No reply. She slammed the heavy receiver back onto its cradle.

Jordan stood in the kitchen waiting for the phone to ring again. It did, but she didn't answer. It stopped ringing, but not ten seconds passed before the cell phone in her pocket began buzzing. The number was restricted.

"Hello?!" she yelled into her phone.

"I will drain every drop of your blood," said the stranger, in the same low, gravelly voice.

"Stop it!" shouted Jordan. She paused, waiting for the stranger to respond.

She was startled when the kitchen phone rang, her cell phone still pressed to her ear. She watched the antique receiver jostle in its cradle as it rang again.

"Answer it!" the stranger growled in her ear.

Jordan picked up the kitchen phone and held it to her other ear.

"Hello?" she said, meekly.

"This is Brother Joseph. You've got to get out of the house!"

Jordan didn't get a chance to respond. A man clad head to toe in black emerged from the back stairs and into the kitchen, tackling her against the countertop. Both phones flew from her hands and smacked against the tile floor.

As she struggled to keep the stranger at bay, she suddenly realized that she hadn't heard the phone ringing from the Colonel's office when Brother Joseph had called. The call from the stranger to her cell phone had been coming from inside the house!

The stranger grabbed her hair and yanked her to the ground. She snatched the old phone from the

134

floor and managed to kick him hard in the shin. She got herself back to her feet by pushing her shoulders against the smooth cupboard door and walking backwards. When the stranger lunged at her again she slammed him in the middle of his black mask with the antique phone receiver. He howled in pain and ran from the kitchen toward the back of the house.

Jordan tore from the kitchen and grabbed Heloise, taking her out the front door and into the night. She didn't know where she was running to, and was about to change direction, when she saw a man coming from the driveway.

"Jordan, what's going on here!?" said the Colonel.

The babysitter was relieved and frantically retold the events that led to her fleeing the house. The Colonel placed her in his car with the keys and told her to the lock the doors. He then retrieved one of his hunting rifles and a pistol from the garage.

She watched the Colonel enter the house, terrified at who he might encounter. She couldn't call the police since her cell phone was still on the floor of the kitchen.

Twenty minutes later, the Colonel returned, to the relief of Jordan and Heloise. He told them to get out of the car, and that he believed it was now safe.

"Someone was in my office rummaging around. They're gone now. I followed a small trail of blood out of the conservatory door, and there are footprints in the mud headed toward the forest."

They returned to the house and Jordan again put Heloise to bed while the Colonel called the detective, whom he had just left an hour prior at the police station.

Melinda the Undead

"*Dies iræ, dies illa, solvet sæclum in favilla. Mors stupebit e natura, cum resurget creatura*," chanted the Colonel, as he read from the Grimoire Scroll. He slaughtered a bound pig before the corpse of his wife, singing the ritual of resurrection and wiping the blood of the hog on an oak stake.

He positioned himself over his dead wife, unholy stake in hand. He plunged the oak spike into her chest and was immediately thrown from the table and onto the floor by some unseen force.

"My God! What have you done?" said Brother Joseph, entering the ballroom in a drunken stupor. The monk had returned to the mansion to assist his friend but had lost track of time, hanging back in the Colonel's office with a '57 Chianti.

The Colonel stood, ignoring the monk, and approached the table to study his wife's lifeless body for any sign that his ritual had worked.

"What have you done?!" reiterated the intoxicated clergyman. The Colonel turned to face him.

"Brother, deeds have been done tonight, many not by my hand, but all with a purpose," stated the Colonel.

The monk looked at him dumbly. The Colonel stared back at him and saw his friend's face contort into a look of utter terror.

"Leave, Brother Joseph." The monk didn't move, just gazed beyond the Colonel at a specter of horror.

The Colonel turned to see his wife sitting up on the table, burial sheet around her waist. She stared at the wall. Her husband came to her and hugged her to him.

"She is risen!" said the Colonel. She tilted her head inhumanly, looking down at his face with a look of contempt.

"Aaahhhh!" screamed the Colonel as his ghoulish wife tore into his jugular vein and neck with her teeth. He grabbed at his severed neck and fell to the table beside her. Again she bit him, shaking her head like a wild wolf as she shredded his flesh.

Brother Joseph looked upon the scene, recoiling from his friend's agony. He slowly turned and slunk toward the ballroom door so as to make his escape. Melinda the Undead rose from her husband's corpse, the unholy stake still lodged in her chest, and began to stalk the monk.

Joseph ran from the ballroom, howling in fear. He jogged up the steps as she gave chase. He darted from room to room, looking for a way out, a weapon, anything to give him more time. However, his inebriation left him in a horrible state in which to make decisions.

Melinda eventually cornered him against a table in the Colonel's library. The fat monk dove over the papers and books, and she leapt onto the table and pinned him.

"Help me!" were the final words spoken by Brother Joseph before he was eviscerated by the teeth and nails of Melinda the Undead.

Jordan had been in the sitting room on the third floor, waiting for her midnight discharge. She ran to the library to when she heard the commotion, and screamed as she entered the room.

Melinda then directed her full attention to Jordan and flew from the table. She chased the babysitter down the hall toward the second floor balcony and fire escape. Jordan had purposely led Melinda away from Heloise's room.

The teenager soon discovered that the balcony door was rusted shut. She went into the closest room and jammed the door with a dresser. It was the Colonel's lavish bedroom. There was a large fireplace in the corner, which she investigated looking for a way out.

Melinda the Undead pounded at the wooden door, eventually breaking the jamb and nudging the dresser enough to get her pale arm through. Jordan went to the window, but saw that it was too high to jump. She returned to the fireplace and grabbed the poker. Melinda had, by then, partially destroyed the door and had moved the dresser enough to allow herself entry.

Jordan spotted the old coal chute and had an idea. She opened it and peered down; it was wide enough for an adult woman. Melinda entered the room and tackled her to the ground. Jordan fought her way back to her feet, hitting and jabbing at her former employer with the iron poker. Melinda lunged at her again as Jordan dove headfirst into the coal chute. The pair tumbled together down the old flue, landing in a pile of wood and coal ash in the basement, Jordan on top of Melinda.

Jordan jumped up, ready for battle. Her shoulder was dislodged and her head ached from smacking around in the passage. A little light shone on the open room from the family crypt's pair of eternal candles. Melinda didn't move. Jordan noticed the stake had gotten dislodged from Melinda's chest and grabbed it to use for a weapon, as the poker had been lost during the fall.

Slowly, Melinda began to sit, the crazed look returning to her face. *Thwack!* Jordan drove the unholy stake into the ghoul's eye socket and was thrown back by the same unseen force that had pushed the Colonel earlier. Melinda then crumpled to the floor, unleashing an unearthly howl as she returned to her former, corpselike state.

Jordan pulled the unholy stake from Melinda's face and stood next to the body, weapon at the ready, waiting for Melinda to rise once again.

The Family Crypt

The babysitter stood in the mansion's basement, her heart racing for a few long minutes. She was startled from her watch when a man appeared from the shadows near the crypt entrance.

"She'll rise again, dear. Better follow me," said Dr. Travis, as he urged the teenage girl to follow him into the family crypt.

Jordan recognized him, but didn't respond, and she didn't know an alternate way out of the dark recesses of the house. She concealed the unholy stake as she trailed the psychiatrist into the dank and noticeably colder tomb passageway. He led her into the main chamber. Generations of the Colonel's family lined the walls, entombed in fine Italian marble. There was a prayer altar in the center of the tomb, with glass cisterns emerging from each end.

The chamber was well lit and she could clearly see the doctor's face in the flickering candlelight. Travis' nose was noticeably broken and he had purple marks on his cheekbones from a concussive force.

He smiled as she put two and two together. She began to back out of the tomb.

"Stay a minute, love," said Dr. Travis, his voice now darker, taking on a gravelly tone that she immediately recognized from their earlier phone conversation.

"What's happening, Dr. Travis?" asked Jordan, her voice trembling.

She continued to tread back toward the passageway. But before she could turn and run, an ornate iron gate slammed behind her, blocking the exit. It was as if the doctor could read her thoughts and had waited until the last second to trap her there.

"Dr. Travis, please…"

"Travis is dead," replied the psychiatrist.

"Who are you?"

The man approached her. "Belial, Servant of Marduk," he replied.

"You killed the Colonel and Melinda?"

Belial shook his head. "I was summoned by the Colonel to fulfill the Prophecy and return Marduk to the living plane."

"The Colonel didn't kill himself, Melinda, Dr. Travis, or Brother Joseph," said Jordan. "You did!"

"Melinda killed Travis before she hanged herself. Travis' death was the conduit I needed to enter the world. The Colonel couldn't have foreseen his wife's madness," explained the demonic entity.

"Are you going to kill me?" asked Jordan, frozen in place.

"No. You are going to help me free my master," said Belial.

"How?" asked Jordan, trying to shake the demon's gaze.

"Your blood and sacrifice on this altar will rebirth Marduk and bring about the Final Epoch," said the demon in a commanding, tomb-shaking tone.

The possessed doctor grabbed her with an unnatural strength, dragging her toward the tomb's altar. Pulled from her gaze, she dropped the unholy stake. Jordan spotted it on the floor and cursed herself for not acting when she had had the chance.

Belial placed her on the altar with a *thud* and she hit her head against one of the water cisterns. The demon raised a dagger to draw her blood, and she flailed and splashed him with water from the nearby cistern. It was a last-ditch effort, and the only thing within reach, but it worked.

"Aaargh!" cried the demon, grabbing his face where the holy water had struck him.

Jordan rolled off the altar and onto the floor, crawling toward the stake near the gated exit. The demon was temporarily blinded and sought her by stomping around the vault and reaching toward the sound of her scurrying away. She reached the unholy stake and grasped it, just as Belial yanked her from the floor and carried her back toward the sacrificial altar.

"Enough of this," growled the demon, disgusted by the holy water.

He tossed her on the altar and retrieved the dagger, intending to cut her from throat to navel. As he raised his arm he left an opening by which she was able to land the unholy stake, and she drove it into the base of his neck above his sternum.

Belial stiffened, dropping his arm and the dagger as he choked up a black, vile ooze. Jordan fell from the altar, thrown by an energy which the demon emitted. A bright flash temporarily blinded the girl, as Belial crumpled into a hot, burning mound of ash before the altar.

Jordan walked off into the night as the Colonel's mansion burned in her wake, the unholy stake and Grimoire Scroll tucked under one arm, young Heloise asleep on her good shoulder.

Regarding Melinda and Dr. Travis' Death and the Note Concealed

An hour prior to Melinda's end, Jordan had heard the woman crying in her boudoir. She knocked cautiously at the door, wary of the unstable woman's response to her presence.

"Yes?" responded Melinda, momentarily stifling her tears.

"It's Jordan. Can I come in?" There was a moment's pause before Melinda consented to the babysitter's entrance.

Melinda's bedroom was lavish, a Victorian period decor. Jordan marveled at the expense of so many antiques, although it was certainly not to her taste. The older woman sat in a chair next to her bed, her hair and makeup a mess from sobbing.

"What's wrong, ma'am?"

"God, I can't believe how screwed up I am," said Melinda, quietly, as the teenager approached.

"What do you mean?"

"Oh, just the way I let men into my life and give them everything—and it's never enough," replied Melinda, wistfully.

"Oh," said Jordan.

Melinda briefly chortled at the girl's response, then she began sobbing. Jordan approached her and hugged her as Melinda remained seated in the chair. She assumed the woman was heartbroken over something her husband might have said to her.

"The Colonel is a dour old man, isn't he?" asked the teenager.

Melinda didn't reply, but she did hand Jordan her letter from Dr. Travis. Jordan sympathetically read the letter while the older woman cried into her hands.

At first, Jordan didn't quite understand the contents of the letter from the psychiatrist—whether it was about the end of a friendship or a professional relationship. But the portion that read, 'My wife is my partner...' was evidence enough that Melinda had been sleeping with her psychiatrist. It infuriated Jordan for many different reasons, one being the fondness she felt for the gruff old Colonel.

"I should go check on Heloise, ma'am," said Jordan, as she excused herself.

Jordan didn't check on her charge after leaving Melinda's bower. She paced the third-floor hallways thinking about the contents of the letter Melinda had received from Dr. Travis. *How could Melinda cheat on her husband with her psychiatrist? How could Travis do such a thing?* she thought, getting herself worked up over the new revelation.

The teenager sat alone in the Colonel's observatory for some time before she was startled from her deep meditation by the entrance of Dr. Travis.

"Hey, I found you," said Dr. Travis, smiling.

"Get lost, asshole," replied Jordan, her eyes wet with tears.

He approached her and she resisted his embrace.

"I broke things off with Melinda because I want to be with you, Jordan," said Travis.

"You're full of shit. You cheated on me with her!" exclaimed Jordan, brusquely.

"I'd leave my wife to be with you. I'm madly infatuated with you, dear," said Travis.

The young girl accepted his embrace as she cried silently, not sure what to do or whom to trust. The months she had given him, all the secret trysts they had shared, were now ruined for her.

At that moment, Melinda appeared in the observatory, curious, having heard Jordan raise her voice. "What the hell, Travis?!" exclaimed an enraged Melinda.

The psychiatrist released the teenager and backed away with his hands in the air.

"Jordan, get back to work," said Melinda, coldly, as Dr. Travis protested.

The teenage girl left the room and heard shouts behind her, mostly coming from her scorned employer. She retrieved Heloise from her room and took her down to the first floor of the mansion.

While Melinda the Deranged stabbed her ex-lover twenty-seven times in the observatory, the Colonel meticulously recited his pledge of fealty to Bel the Resurrected in the library on the floor below. He had been in full mastery of the power of the scroll, and was too deep into his rituals to notice the psychiatrist's faint screaming.

AN EPISTLE FROM THE DEAD

Regina Fleck had buried her remarkable husband, Thomas Fleck, in a most remarkable mausoleum. She had been full of pride during his eulogy (it was given by a state supreme court justice) and terrified at the prospect of a future without him. Days had passed since, and she sat with his objects in his study, in remembrance of him.

After looking through his desk and fingering his personal effects, Regina noticed the loosely bound manuscript, pulled it out and began to read.

This would resemble my diary, had it been written.

As a child, I watched a cat slowly die of dehydration. For days, I'd go into the woods behind my parents' home and listen to the cat cry. It was stuck in a drainage well and couldn't turn its body. I was amazed at its will to survive. On the fourth day, it rained heavily. The cat drowned.

Regina sat with the neatly written series of pages, familiar with the handwriting. She didn't know what to make of the first few pages. The text seemed more a story told than a life lived.

147

At school, I helped my teachers at their menial tasks, often staying well past the final bell. The other kids resented how they favored me. I would rummage through the personal possessions of the adults and children, study the comment cards and grade books. I didn't do it for test advantage, but to study the performance, punishments, and laurels of my peers. I needed to know each and every other intimately. My entire life had been dedicated to knowing yet concealing.

Regina became uneasy and went to her kitchen for a drink, still clutching the papers. She skipped down the page (advancing the age of her husband) and began reading again.

My first romantic attachments were to a neighborhood girl, and a boy a year my elder who was employed by my father's gardener. My time spent with the weed puller caused the girl great consternation. She was sent to a facility for treatment, and of her prospects following I've no knowledge. She was the closest I've ever felt to love.

The young man's purpose to me was solely to cause jealousy. Once he was of no use, I prodded him to reveal himself to his father. He was severely beaten and I haven't thought of him again until this moment.

Regina trembled as she skipped to the middle of the following page. Why would Thomas write such things?

I was attracted to Regina for her simplemindedness. I knew early on she wouldn't delve too deeply into who I was. The more of me I hid from her, the more in control I felt. She wasn't fit to mother. I knew she'd struggle every hour caring for anything other than herself...

There was knocking at the front door, but it barely registered for Regina. She skimmed the

148

passages that dealt with her, thinking of her virginity, childbirth, marriage. All of the great joys of her life were now tarnished.

When I entered the public sphere, it was only to serve my own ends. To be thought of as an environmentalist was of less advantage than I imagined. The reason I protected those stinking swamps from being paved and planted was only to put Arthur Brooks into Chapter 11. To my last day, I will hold his destitution and demise as my greatest work.

Regina shook visibly, thinking of all the splendid dinners she had organized for the Audubon and other various foundations that she and Thomas had sat for. The knocking at the front door grew more insistent, but she was too caught up in the horror of her husband's text. It continued, describing the tax advantages of building a homeless shelter on one of the most chemically polluted sites in the county. She made a mental note to ask her staff about rates of cancer among those living at the shelter.

I would have as easily tossed my children into the river at birth, as I merely mimed the role of father, nurturer, and provider. They certainly brought me no joy in their middling triumphs, nor any worry in their mundane defeats. How could a man love or cherish anything less than his measure? These adult children of mine: teacher, firefighter, family attorney, nonprofit executive...

She couldn't finish her husband's confession. She wept uncontrollably and tore the text into dozens of shredded strips, and then into miniscule bits and pieces, tossing them into the sink and running the disposal. A heavy crunching sound filled the quiet home. All the while, someone was still banging on the front door.

Regina returned to her husband's study, ignoring the rapping at the door, and retrieved the revolver from his desk. Her hand, as if disassociated from her person, placed the barrel to her mouth and ended her life—just days after her remarkable husband's remarkable funeral.

* * *

Thomas Fleck Jr. sat and mourned with his brother and two sisters after their mother's funeral. It was all too much for the siblings—two funerals and two parents gone within two weeks' time.

"Tom, how could she?! Oh, the fact that you were *just outside*," wailed his youngest sister, Alison.

"I'd forgotten the key in my excitement," replied Tom. The schoolteacher had already told the story countless times. Holding *The New Yorker* in hand with his recently published story. Spotting his mother's car in the driveway. Knowing she was home; so happy to share his success with her in the midst of her mourning. And then the horror of the gunshot.

"I know it would have made her so proud to see your first story published, Tom," said Jennifer, his eldest sister, the attorney.

"I wanted it to be a surprise. I'd only shown Dad, since it was such a black portrayal of someone of his stature. It was such a sloppy draft, before I'd even changed all the names. His feedback was really

150

what inspired me to finish and submit it," said Tom, openly weeping with his siblings. "I would have loved for Mom to have read it. She had such a fondness for fiction."

PICTURES OF A PERPETUAL SUBJECT

The elm in Johanna's backyard was bare, fitting the season. The tree was a pleasing sight year-round—regardless of its decor, no more or less immutable than the season before. Johanna often looked out her bedroom's big bay window and admired the tree's natural splendor; it was a raw, clockwork beauty in a world consumed by materialistic self-obsession.

Johanna set her camera up on a small tripod overlooking her backyard, the tree taking center stage in the frame. She made sure the tripod was steady and the camera secure, as she would be taking the same photo every day for a year and wanted a consistent shot. The idea to construct a photo essay had struck her after an incident at school. A group of nasty girls had taken a photo of her in the hallway then doctored the image, widening her hips and expanding her already disproportionately large breasts. The entire class had passed the photo around via text message and social media.

Rather than exact some kind of revenge on the girls, or to hide herself in shame, Johanna instead chose to use her energy to highlight something true, something outside of herself. Her classmates spent most of their time on their smartphones and in front of their computers, consuming and producing photos, video, and text of and about themselves. Johanna thought of all of the viral videos she had seen showing the change of one individual through daily selfies. Instead of taking her own photo for a year, she would turn the camera outward and reveal a part of herself beyond the cosmetic.

The Kodak company offered a photo essay scholarship every year and she was going to enter her project the following year. The elm in her backyard had been there before her time and, she thought, would likely still be standing there long after. She held a deep respect for its permanence and thought it made the perfect subject for her project.

She looked through the viewfinder at the scene outside. Beyond her fenced-in backyard lay a small, overgrown field which bordered the town cemetery. She watched as tiny people in the distance got out of their cars and approached a burial tent. When she had finally found the perfect shot—the tree centered, the cemetery in the background—she snapped her first photo. "Day one," she said, smiling.

Johanna delighted in her daily ritual. The tree, with its old, cracking bark and wide, hulking trunk, struck a poignant image. After three months had passed, she decided to review the status of her project. She removed the memory card from her camera and plugged it into her computer, compiling all the photos into one thirty-second video clip, and pressed 'play.' Vibrant, yellow leaves appeared on the branches; the grass took on a livelier shade of green; people and cars appeared in the cemetery beyond. But the tree remained still, untroubled by the world. She liked that about it.

She was smiling, happy with the way the video was turning out, until she noticed a small blotch that appeared near the end. Curious, she replayed the video. The blotch appeared in the background then grew slightly larger. She looked through the individual photos to see which were the cause of the blemish, but noticed nothing. The blotch, strangely, was only visible when she played the video.

Without removing her camera from the tripod, she inspected the lens for any possible smears or smudges. Maybe, she thought, a speck of dust or dirt had landed on the lens and slid across. But she found no such obstruction. She hoped the blotch had just been a temporary digital glitch and would not interfere with her project in the months to come.

For the next several weeks she took her daily photos, and when she reached the six-month mark, she made another video of the previous three months' photos in succession. The leaves turned a lush green, and she thought of all of the summers she had played in the yard under the shade of the tree.

Johanna hadn't noticed the figure appear in the cemetery on first viewing, as she was so enthralled by the changing of the tree.

When she combined all six months' worth of photos and played the video, she realized that the blotch had been a person, and that person was coming toward her backyard! She was astonished, as she had been taking individual still photos, roughly a day apart, and the figure appeared to be walking in her direction, almost as if she had recorded an actual short video.

Johanna searched through each of the ninety or so stills to find any evidence of the blotch or the figure in the graveyard. Nothing. She walked down the hall to grab her brother, Jonathan, who was home from college. She brought him into her room and sat him down in front of her computer.

"Jon, you've got to watch this video and tell me what you see in the background," said Johanna. She pressed play and waited for his reaction.

Jon watched intently for the full minute. "What am I looking for?"

"Do you see someone walking in the cemetery?"

"Uh, maybe. Play it back again."

Johanna replayed the video. Beneath the branches of the elm, the blotch grew and then clearly became a figure walking in the camera's direction. Although she knew it was coming, she found it no less unsettling.

"Okay, I see someone walking and it's a pretty neat video—but what's the point?"

"Jon, these are *still* images that I've been taking once a day for the past six months. There's no way there could be a person walking in the same exact spot every day," replied Johanna.

Jon chuckled and clicked one of the stills near the end, filling the screen with the image. He looked confused, as there was no figure in it. "Huh? So you just took a video, then?"

Johanna shook her head. "The person doesn't appear in the stills, just when I make it a video. It doesn't make sense."

Jonathan laughed as if she was pulling a prank on him, and returned to his room. Johanna sat in front of her computer, playing the video over and over, trying to come up with a rational explanation for the strange figure.

Her mother wandered in at one point and silently stood at the window, staring out at the backyard.

"What's up, Mom?" mumbled Johanna, still concentrating on the video in front of her. Her mother lingered as if she wanted to say something, but soon left, likely recalling a forgotten task.

Johanna continued her daily photos, anticipating the destination of the figure within. When another three months had passed, she again took the stills and anxiously uploaded them to her computer. She played the video and waited.

Green leaves disappeared from the tree and the ground become brown and then white, but Johanna hardly noticed any of the seasonal changes; her attention was focused solely on the erratic movements of the ghostly figure. She watched as the thing climbed the fence and set foot in her backyard. The ghoul was oddly distorted compared to the surrounding landscape, but she could make out some discernible features: long, dark hair and what appeared to be a white dress. The video ended just as the figure began to advance toward her house.

The door to Johanna's bedroom suddenly opened, causing her to gasp.

"Mom!" yelled Johanna. "Could you knock?!"

Her mom peeked into her room and sighed. "Oh, Jo-Jo."

"It's alright, Mom," said Johanna. The image of the mysterious figure fresh on her mind, she actually found her mother's presence a relief, especially since her brother was away at college. "I'm just busy—" Before she could finish her thought, her mom left, shutting the door behind her.

Johanna watched the video again, nervously considering what it meant for the ghoul to enter her family's domain. Again, she checked the images individually, and saw no evidence of an approaching figure.

She looked over at the camera as it sat in front of the window. What would appear in the next video? she wondered. If she continued to take photos, would she see the figure move even closer— perhaps even come to her *window*? She stood up nervously and looked outside. There was no discernible evidence that anyone had been in the backyard that morning—the snow was untouched save for the footprints of small game. There was no explanation for what she was witnessing when she ran her day-to-day stills together, and this unknown filled her with trepidation. Johanna unscrewed the camera from the tripod and placed it in her bag, deciding that she already had enough to worry about in her daily life.

But when she thought back to school—to the taunts, the crass concerns of her peers—she realized that she couldn't give up. The photo study was too important an undertaking for her to end over some irrational fear. So she took the camera back out of the bag, screwed it back on the tripod, and set it up to capture the same image. Whoever or whatever the figure was, she was going to finish her project and bear witness to the ghoul's intention.

Every day for the next three months Johanna dealt with her anxiety, walking to her bedroom window and shooting a photo of the tree and its surroundings. Finally, on the one-year anniversary of her project, she snapped the final picture and went to her computer to watch the last three months unfold. With a near-paralyzing dread, she compiled the full video and pushed play. There, as clear as the waning snow and newly minted red leaves, was the approaching figure. The scenery changed and the sky took on various shades with each passing day, but the ghoul was a constant. It worked its way from the cemetery to the fence, climbing it and entering her family's backyard. She shuddered as the final three months of stills began with the ghoul now seemingly advancing with purpose toward her bedroom window. Johanna was shocked when the figure abruptly turned toward the tree and began to climb it.

She lost sight of the figure as it ascended the tree and was obscured by the leaves. She shot a quick look out her window at the tree, expecting to catch a real-world glimpse of something—moving branches, a flash of the white dress—but she saw nothing out of the ordinary.

Johanna turned her attention back to the video. She sat, shaking, and watched the remaining stills flash by, momentarily thinking that the ghoul had vanished, when suddenly, the figure in white dropped below the lowest branches, grotesquely swaying with each successive still, seemingly hanging by its neck. But there was no rope in view.

Johanna cried as the video ended, unable to process the horrific image she had witnessed. She ran out of her room and down the hallway. She screamed her brother's name as she pounded on his door.

"What?!" exclaimed Jonathan, coming out of his room.

Johanna frantically described to him what she had just watched, and he seemed to look at her in pity. She dragged him back to her bedroom and was about to play the video when he stopped her.

"What are you doing, Jon? You have to see this. It's really freaky."

"Jo, open up the first image," he said, wearily. "Check the date."

"Why?" Johanna was confused. She was certain there would be no evidence of the hanging ghoul in the early stills, the same as there was nothing of the figure in any of the more recent pictures.

"Please, just do it."

Johanna double-clicked the first photo. She was shocked to see the file was named "November 25, 2015." "Huh? I don't get it. I took that photo last year. Why is it today's date?"

Jonathan sighed, then looked at his sister morosely. "Because that's the day you died…"

She looked at her brother, horrified that he'd make such a dumb joke when she was trying to figure out a real-life mystery. "That's not funny, Jon. There's a ghost in our backyard, and I think it's important for all of us that we figure out why."

"Jo, today's date is November 25, *2019*. Click on the photo you took today."

She obediently opened the file for the picture she had taken that morning. "November 25, *2014*." She cocked her head to the side and looked at the date curiously.

Johanna smirked at her older brother, trying to figure out his angle. "Okay, let me go online and see what today's date is…" She went to a few news sites, and sure enough, it was November 25, 2019. "I-I…really don't understand what's happening, Jon."

"Johanna, check the dates on the pictures you took yesterday and the day before…"

She clicked on them and, oddly enough, they were dated November 26, 2014 and November 27, 2014. "Why aren't they in the order I took them?"

"They are, Johanna." Jon opened the video again, reversing it and pressing 'play.'

She focused intently as the full video played; no ghoul emerged from the graveyard nor entered her backyard, and nothing but leaves fell from the tree. "Jon, why is there no ghost now?"

"Jo, did you notice how the seasons seemed to change in a different order than in your version?"

She nodded. "They weren't in the right order before..."

"I'm sorry, Johanna. This is the fifth time you've done this photo project and the fourth time I've had to explain to you that you're no longer living. You killed yourself the same day you finished your photo essay, and for some reason you've been repeating it year after year."

Johanna began silently weeping as Jon continued. "Jo, remember when you used to drive me to school? You were three years older than *me* when you died. I've aged and you've stayed the same. And did you notice that you haven't had a conversation with Mom in the past year? She can't see or hear you."

She thought back to the last year. It was true; she had not had an in-depth conversation with her mother, but she had never really thought about it. And Jonathan *did* look suddenly older. She searched her mind for a rational explanation, anything that could disprove her brother's wild claims, but she knew it was futile. She resigned herself to his explanation; she knew it was true.

"What happens now, Jon?"

"Can you remember the day that you died? I've asked you year after year to remember that day and to please explain why you hanged yourself."

"Jon, I- I- can't remember... Oh, god. What's happening to me?!" She lifted her arm and saw that it had become incorporeal, an almost hazy outline of what was once her limb.

"Jo, I want you to know that I did submit your photo essay to the contest. You won. Mom was really proud and they ended up giving me the scholarship in your name." A tear streamed down Jonathan's cheek in what had become an annual moment of anguish.

Johanna hugged her brother. "I'm not going to remember this, am I?"

"I'm sorry, Jo. But I'll see you soon..."

With that, Johanna faded from the material world.

Outside, the elm tree swayed in the autumn breeze.

ACKNOWLEDGMENTS

We'd like to thank the following people for their encouragement and (endless) patience: Burt for providing us with indispensable critique yet again, Chad for designing an evocative cover, the Speculative Writers of the Southern Tier for being great allies in the macabre, Sybil for the living room—and our always calm and never distracting children.

MORE ODD AND MACABRE TALES

"The authors have crafted seventeen stories of intelligent, moody, and grim horror while connecting the tales with their own rich history."
—**Nightmare News Network**

FROM BRHEL & SULLIVAN

"A delightfully entertaining paranormal, supernatural, magical set of vignettes, tied inextricably to
the illustrious Dr. Marvelry, and his gently eccentric
boutique."
—The Haunted Reading Room

79572426R00102

Made in the USA
Columbia, SC
04 November 2017